About the Author

Susan Price won the Carnegie Medal for *Ghost Drum* in 1987 and was shortlisted again in 1994 for *Head and Tales*. She writes: 'I was born in a slum in Oldbury, West Midlands – no bathroom or running water inside; an outside lavatory shared with several other house-holds; and cockroaches and mice. But we got a council house when I was four, and moved about a mile away, nearer to Dudley, where I still live.

I have a pet, a little grey tabby cat with white patches. She has beautiful pale green eyes, with a black line round them, as if she is wearing mascara. I like sharing my house with another kind of animal. I always have to share my chair with her. Tig's usually curled up somewhere near me while I'm writing.'

Also published by Hodder Children's Books

Earthfasts
Cradlefasts
William Mayne

Foundling
June Oldham

Waterbound
Jane Stemp

Brother Cat, Brother Man
Zoe Halliday

HAUNTINGS

SUSAN PRICE

Hodder
Children's
Books

a division of Hodder Headline plc

A Catalogue record for this book is available from the
British Library

ISBN 0 340 62655 0

Typeset by
Phoenix Typesetting, Ilkley, W. Yorkshire

Printed and bound in Great Britain by
Cox & Wyman Ltd, Reading, Berks.

Hodder Children's Books
a division of Hodder Headline plc
338 Euston Road
London NW1 3BH

Contents

Gosling

Delamare had shaved, dressed and perfumed himself, and was now sitting at his dressing table, masking blemishes with a little face powder, and touching the edges of his eyes with kohl. If you were going to meet the public, he reasoned, you should be more beautiful than they were – not a difficult task, most of the time. Especially you should look beautiful if you wanted them to believe you.

He was wiping away kohl with a wisp of cotton wool, until only the subtlest, most natural-seeming darkening of his lash-line remained, when the telephone rang. He lifted the receiver. 'Yes?'

It was Ogden, speaking on the internal line. 'We've got a new 'un.' Ogden had no ear, and had never been able to do more than slightly modify his accent.

'Oh, goodie.' Delamare was gazing at himself in the mirror. His hairline was retreating, but only gave him a higher, nobler brow, and, having always been fair, the grey hardly showed. Instead of wrinkling him, age seemed to have worn his thin face smoother, making the cheekbones higher, the nose more aristocratically thin and beaky. 'Who else has turned up?'

'Your usuals. Annie Shepherd—'

'Oh, that fat old walking jumble sale.'

'Paul Dorking—'

'A bag of dust in a suit.' Delamare was pleased to hear Ogden laugh. 'Have you put out his file for me?'

'Of course.'

'I shall have to look up his mother and wife – never a pretty sight.' He earned another laugh. 'I always mix up their names.'

'And there's Julie Banks, Mr and Mrs Fletcher, Alan Dean—'

'Oh, yes, all the usuals. I'm getting stale. A new one, you say? Do expound.'

'I've never seen him before, and none of the others seem to know him – but he signed the visitors' book, "S. Gosling", for what that's worth.'

'How old?'

'Thirties, pretending to be twenties, I'd say.'

Ogden's tone amused Delamare. 'Oh? Pretty?'

'Chinless.'

'Oh, *that* pretty.' Delamare laughed. 'Well, earn your keep, Oggie. Tell 'em I need fifteen minutes to commune with the spirits and go and offer them refreshments while they wait. Get me something to go on.'

Delamare spent the time by reading through the files

Ogden had left on the smooth, dark-blue coverlet of his bed. He and Ogden had, over the years, compiled obituaries from newspapers, scraps of local gossip and the trivia of chit-chat recorded in their bugged waiting room, and their files held an astonishing amount of information about their clients' private lives. Family members, alive and dead; pets, alive and dead, their names, types and habits; hobbies, dreams, nightmares, ambitions, holidays, favourite colours, marital difficulties, operations and illnesses – nothing was so unimportant that it couldn't be used to amaze and convince.

About ten minutes later, Ogden, a big fleshy man who had long outgrown and outeaten his prettiness, came up with the tape from the waiting-room recorder. 'Our Annie's got another bee in her bonnet.' Delamare looked up from the file he was reading, and Ogden explained, 'Seances can attract elementals as well as spirits, y'know. An elemental might have attached itself to her and followed her home.'

'It's the only thing that's likely to follow her home, poor old duck. Who's she been talking to?'

'It's something she's been reading, I think.'

Delamare sighed, and tossed the file on to the bed. 'I do wish she'd remember she's stupid, and not attempt difficult things like reading. What about our newcomer?'

Ogden paused for a moment as he fitted the tape on to the machine beside Delamare's bed. 'He's trouble.'

'How's that?'

'He's a reporter, I'll put money on it. Too clever by half. He won't talk. Ask him where he comes from and it's, "oh, around". Ask him what he does – "oh, nothing interesting".'

'Perhaps he's shy,' Delamare said, mainly to annoy Ogden, but aware of his own, slight, wishfulness.

'Shy, my armhole. He's here to catch you out, Del. He's been put up to it.'

'Well,' Delamare said, 'we can't always have it all our own way, can we? Let's start.'

He knew that everything was in place, ready and working, because he'd checked it all himself; but he suddenly wished that he could check it again. He always felt a pleasurable fear before a performance, but, with the knowledge that there would be an unbeliever in his audience, the fear was less pleasurable. His stomach felt queasy.

He made himself smile. 'Let's convert young Chin-less.' It was tempting fate, but it made him feel more confident. Tempting fate always did. He'd got away with it so often in the past.

The seances were held in the front room of the house, with black curtains drawn across the windows. The walls had been draped in black cloth, but Delamare was still aware of the mundane picture-rails and skirting boards, the flowery, damp-yellowed wallpaper hidden by the drapes, and entering the room always gave him a twinge of irritation.

His clients turned as he entered, and rose from their chairs, their movements releasing whiffs of tobacco, wet wool and dogs. They were a drab lot, the men in cheap grey or navy-blue suits, the women in depressingly prim black skirts and white blouses, or baggy beige dresses. The deliberately dim lighting of the room, from heavily shaded lamps and an electric candelabra with flame-shaped bulbs, drained the colours and made them even uglier, while emphasising every sag and bag of the faces. Delamare had made sure that the lighting which fell on his chair, on its little dais, was much more flattering.

'Good evening to you all, good evening,' Delamare said, spreading his hands to encompass them all in his greeting. He smiled, well able to be soft-spoken and modest, because he knew they acknowledged him as their superior – well, all but young Chinless, per-haps. Delamare didn't look for him yet, deliberately delaying and savouring the moment when he would first meet him. 'I'm so sorry to keep you all waiting, but I felt so tired this evening – it's taken me such a long time to raise my energy.'

Annie Shepherd, her fat little face glowing, her eyes shining with all the love and admiration she felt for him, reached out both thick hands towards him and cried, 'Oh, Mr Delamare, that might be the elementals! You have to take care of yourself, Mr Delamare – for our sakes – you really must take care of yourself!'

They had all gathered around him – except one, on the edge of his vision, who remained seated – and they were all beaming at him with the same fatuous, trusting devotion. Delamare loved it. Kindly he took Annie's hand.

'Why, Miss Shepherd, it's so good of you to be concerned for me. But what's this? Elementals?'

She blushed with pleasure at his touch and his affectionate tone, and looked up and down and everywhere but at his face. For a moment, Delamare almost liked her.

'Elementals, Mr Delamare – oh, *you* know! You would attract them, I'm sure! Like flies to honey!'

The people standing near her shifted, and nodded, and murmured agreement.

Delamare was still holding Annie's hand, and he pressed it slightly. 'But who's been worrying you with elementals, Miss Shepherd?'

She raised her black eyes to his face, hastily looked away, and giggled. 'Oh, I've been reading – I like to inform myself. But I don't want to set myself up as knowing—! I mean, you must know – oh, so much more!'

'You've read that elementals are attracted to seances, is that it?' Delamare asked.

The others were beginning to become restive, with so much of Delamare's attention focussed on Annie. Alan Dean, a large youth who always seemed hot and damp, asked, 'What are elementals?'

And Paul Dorking cleared his throat, as he always did before speaking, and said, 'Low-level spirits.' He looked sideways to check that Delamare approved of his answer. 'Tricksy, malicious things, quite unpredictable and dangerous.'

'Unpredictable and dangerous!' Annie cried, widening her eyes. 'They could be why you're feeling so tired, Mr Delamare!' She turned her wide eyes on the people near her. 'And they could attach themselves to any one of us!'

'Annie, Annie,' Delamare said gently, giving her hands a little shake. 'As Mr Dorking says, elementals are simple things. Only a very simple and inexperienced practitioner could be in danger from them, and I'm not that! I assure you that my psychic guards are quite strong enough to protect all of us from such simple things as elementals.'

'But after the sitting last week,' she said, 'I heard such funny noises coming from my back kitchen. I was sure something had followed me home.'

Delamare laughed. It was a carefully judged laugh:

13

not scornful, but warm, calculated to make Annie feel girlish and silly, but comforted. He cocked his head on one side to look at her. 'Imagination, Miss Shepherd, imagination.' She looked shocked, and he went on, 'Far be it from me to dismiss everything we can't understand as imagination, but, you know, especially sensitive people such as yourself must be on their guard against their very vivid imaginations.'

The compliment made Annie lower her eyes again, her face blushing.

'I do assure you, Miss Shepherd, that at my seances no harm can come to you, or me, or anyone.'

Paul Dorking coughed and said, 'I never doubted it.'

'It'd be well worth the risk anyway,' someone else said.

Delamare spread his hands graciously. 'You are all too kind; I don't deserve you.' He was happy to keep the homage coming as they plainly enjoyed paying it as much as he did spooning it up. But Ogden didn't share in the homage, and cut it short.

'We have a new member tonight, Delamare. May I introduce—?'

From the corner of his eyes, Delamare saw the seated figure rising to meet him, and allowed himself to turn in that direction at last, holding out his hand and saying, 'Ah, Mr Gosling! So pleased to meet you!'

In the past his greeting of a newcomer by name had evoked surprise, which made it easier to convince them of his other powers. The fact that they had signed a visitors' book in the presence of his assistant had often slipped their minds. This young man, however, met his eyes with an appreciative but rather knowing smile and no surprise at all. 'And I to meet you, Mr Delamare.'

Delamare felt some disappointment at the failure of his trick, but, for once, none in Gosling's appearance. Ogden's description had been more than a little unfair. Even the lighting which made everyone else look old and plain couldn't spoil Gosling. His very dark hair and pale skin made a vivid contrast that couldn't be drained, and the shadows emphasised the sharpness of his nose and cheekbones. A triangular face with a narrow, pointed chin which, yes, was perhaps a little weak – but the unflattering light could throw no more than the faintest shadow under his eye and at the corner of his mouth. He might have been as young as twenty-five, except that a certain firmness of face and manner, a certain gauntness of the cheeks suggested that he was older. But, with his very straight black brows, and very dark eyes, he was a pretty young man, a very pretty young man indeed.

'May I ask, do you have any special reason for joining our group, Mr Gosling?'

Gosling smiled slightly, and Delamare was fascinated by his own reflection, and the reflection of a flame-shaped bulb, in the steady, bright, dark eyes. That pointed face, that fine, foxy nose and those bright, dark eyes – 'the woodland creature' would be a perfect name for him, Delamare thought.

So fascinated was he that he realised with a start that Gosling had finished speaking, and he was still staring into his eyes. What had the young man said? From his memory of a few seconds before, Delamare caught, 'No special reason.' And something about having a general interest in the after-life . . . And Gosling was still smiling the kind of polite but guarded smile people use when being evasive. A very taking smile. It made him look gentler and younger, but showed his upper teeth rather prominently in a sharp, narrow arc. It gave him an even more squirrelish look.

And that voice. It was almost as perfectly accentless as Delamare's, but not quite. It had slipped, and 'life' had come out as 'loife'. They were perfectly charming, these little imperfections, the not-quite-perfect accent, the slightly bucked teeth, and Delamare felt a spurt of affection for this fellow deceiver. I could teach you, he thought, to talk as if your daddy was a duke, and you could use those teeth on my lip.

Remembering himself, he said warmly, 'You're like our Mr Dean – interested in the life hereafter while still young enough to feel immortal! Do let me introduce you: Alan Dean and—?'

'Saul Gosling.'

Delamare watched as the two young men shook hands: Dean, tall, heavy-bodied, fair-haired; and Gosling, slight, pale and dark. Gosling, it seemed to Delamare, couldn't keep a certain irony out of his smile and manner, a certain aloofness. To be certain, Delamare introduced him to the others and watched him with them. And no, he concluded, the little woodland creature was not a believer. His manner, taken with his evasive replies and Ogden's doubts, convinced Delamare completely. Nor was he a sightseer, come out of curiosity to giggle – sightseers come in couples, or even threes or fours, not alone. No, the woodland creature was, as Ogden had said, trouble. More fox than squirrel.

None of the others, of course, had noticed anything. They were welcoming Gosling with all the enthusiasm of a small elect thinking they have found another supporter. It made Delamare smile to see Annie Shepherd disguising her attraction to the young man as motherliness and inviting him to, 'Sit between me and Mrs Fletcher, love, so you'll feel at home.'

While they were still talking, Delamare made his way round them to his chair, on its small raised platform at the other end of the room. He seated himself in his usual pose, back quite straight, feet together, and arms resting on the arms of his chair – the pose of an Egyptian god-king in a sculpture. Paul Dorking was the first to notice that Delamare had taken his place – he usually was – and he quickly conveyed this, by looks and light touches, to the others. Conversations were broken off, and they hurriedly took their own seats. It pleased Delamare to see them so obedient to his unspoken will. So much more gratifying than if he had to call them to order.

He watched Saul Gosling being chivvied to his chair in motherly fashion by Annie Shepherd and Mrs Fletcher. The young man was looking about the room and, in his bright-eyed, prick-eared woodland-creature way he noted, Delamare was sure, what no one else took much notice of – the fact that Ogden quietly left the room.

Delamare continued to sit, without speaking, staring unseeingly before him, until the expectant quiet of his audience became deeply, velvetly hushed. At the blurred edge of his vision he was aware of Gosling watching him with close attention, and he was careful not to glance that way. Wait a while, my lad, he thought, we'll see if you don't end by watching me with as much respect as poor old Annie does.

'I must ask you to be very quiet and still, ladies and gentlemen,' he said, keeping his voice low to make them listen. 'I am about to go into trance, and my concentration must be unbroken.'

The silence, to Delamare's delight, became more hushed yet, as they stilled every muscle and even held their breath.

Delamare allowed himself to go limp, let his head sag on to his shoulders. He made his breathing harsh and heavy, even moaned a little. The knowledge that Gosling was listening sceptically, perhaps even smiling, pricked him on to a virtuoso performance, with moans more hollow and wrenching than he'd produced for months. His regulars were so easily satisfied. When he finally allowed his head and shoulders to slump forwards, the silence was so deep and yet so prickly with awe, that he almost smiled himself. He should make the effort to put on a top-class show more often. It was good for him.

He wished that he could sneak a look at young Gosling. Had the heart-rending moans shaken him? Was he sitting up and paying attention? Delamare found, a little to his own surprise, that he hoped not. The thought of the bright-eyed little woodland creature, with his charmingly fake accent and his slightly bucked teeth, being absorbed into the dull ranks of Annie Shepherd, Alan Dean and Paul Dorking, depressed him. It was churlish perhaps, but he had only condescension, edged with contempt, for those who believed in his powers.

Slowly he raised his head, his eyes closed, breathing slowly and deeply. Watch me, he was thinking at Gosling: watch me and see what you think of this.

His voice, when he spoke, was flatter and pitched a little deeper than usual. 'I am here,' he said, in an accent he had learned, years ago, from a Polish friend. 'There are many who wish to speak with the living,' said the Polish voice, and there was a happy sigh from those listening.

There, thought Delamare: have you ever heard a more perfect imitation of a Pole? Couldn't I iron out those little slips in your accent? It would be almost a shame, though – 'loife'! Charming!

Must concentrate. Drop the Polish accent, adopt a local one, pitch the voice a little higher and sweeter – 'Annie! You're a good girl! Always remember I love you.'

He heard a little rustle, the little whimper from Annie and felt that warm sympathy he only felt for her at such times, the sympathy of the cat for the mouse. Poor woman: too ugly to marry, only spinster daughter of deceased parents, these weekly assurances from her dead mother – speaking what the mother had probably never said while alive – were the only affection she received. Delamare never forgot to give her those words and it paid. She came back every week, always left a little donation, and was his best advertisement.

Another change of voice: a more refined accent, a softer tone – but he wouldn't have put so much effort into it if it hadn't been for the unbeliever in the audience. 'Paul – waiting for you always, dearest.'

Softly he heard Paul Dorking's whispered, convinced reply, 'I'll be coming soon, dearest.'

Now for a change. Doubt this, he thought at Gosling: doubt your own ears. From a corner of the room behind his audience came a trembling shower of bell-sound. A new effect. He kept his eyes closed, but heard his audience twisting round in their chairs and gasping. They fell silent again as the shimmering bells faded, and there rose instead the awe-inspiring sound of a Russian choir, all swaying basses and soaring sopranos.

The audience listened raptly, until the singing ended, which it did a little too abruptly for Delamare's liking. Surely, he thought, wincing, Gosling would have noticed that. Badly managed, badly managed. If he'd have known that he was going to have someone so much worth convincing in the audience, he'd have taken more care with that.

But never mind – the lamps. First the lamp in the far corner. He made it go out. The sudden thickening and reaching out of shadows made people gasp, and turn towards the darkness. Like children being told a fairy-tale, they always cooed and gasped, even though they knew it was going to happen. It was what they wanted to have happen. But Delamare wished he could open his eyes and see Gosling's face.

Put out all the lamps, he thought, even the candelabra. He made it happen. Complete darkness dropped on the room. Chairs creaked, clothes rustled, harsh breaths were drawn as the audience shifted. He made one lamp come on again. For his next trick, he didn't want too much illumination.

From the shadows of the high ceiling something fluttered down, white and very faintly luminous in the frail light from the single, shaded lamp. It was an effect that Delamare didn't use too often, in case familiarity spoiled it. A muslin ghost, drifting in the air over their heads, humming faintly as it moved, to the glorious music of the Russian choir.

Annie Shepherd said, sharply, 'What—?' Delamare smiled to himself, pleased to have made old Annie jump – and after all the seances she'd seen! But then she said, 'What you doing?' And other voices too – exclaiming, saying, 'Hey!' Delamare felt alarm. The voices had the wrong tone – they weren't awed. They were shocked.

He opened his eyes. He saw Gosling standing and reaching up. Just as Gosling's hand closed on the muslin of the ghost's skirt, Delamare turned off even the single lamp.

Darkness, and a noise of chairs being pushed back, of people rising. 'What're you playing at?' Alan Dean's voice demanded. Annie was squeaking something, distressed; and there was a general hub-bub of surprise and indecision.

Then Gosling's voice came from the darkness, a voice a little breathless and touched with a nervousness that made an immediate appeal to Delamare. 'Come on,' Gosling said. 'You may as well turn the loights back on.' The failure of the acquired accent conquered Delamare. What the hell, he thought. I might as well give in with style. He switched on all the lamps and the main candelabra; and then leaned back in his chair, and crossed his legs, his eyes open and his fingers steepled.

Gosling held the muslin ghost between his hands, displaying it to the others. He looked up, and the others copied him. There were the rods that moved the ghost. Usually hidden against the black-painted ceiling, they were now in full, if somewhat shadowed view.

Gosling lowered his head and looked Delamare directly in the face, his own face amused. His eyes were very bright, and his face had flushed, losing some of its paleness. 'Electricity,' he said, his fake accent back in place. 'Concealed pressure pads – in the arms of the chair and under the rug.' He stepped up on to the dais, right beside Delamare, and pressed the rug with the toe of his shoe, at first without success. Delamare watched calmly.

'What you playing at?' Alan Dean demanded again, growing impatient with Gosling's efforts. Dean's face was swollen, his fists were clenched, and he glared at Gosling. It occurred to Delamare that he might have to intercede to save his little woodland creature from the much beefier Dean's anger. He hoped so.

'There!' Gosling said, as his toe at last found a pressure pad, and the lamp on the table by the window went out. He pressed again, and it came back on. Gosling turned and looked at Dean triumphantly, grinning his narrow, squirrelly grin.

'Well, what's that prove?' Dean said, getting angrier. Delamare shook his head slightly. The others just stood, and stared. Dorking swallowed with difficulty.

Gosling knelt at the edge of the dais and turned back the rug to show the little rubber pads and the wires. Looking up at Dean, he said, 'All the effects are done by electricity. Didn't you hear the tape run down when the singing stopped? It was a tape-recording. He switched it off by using one of these contacts – or one in the chair arm. You could see his fingers and feet moving if you were watching for it.'

So quickly that he made a breeze, Paul Dorking turned and walked out of the room, head up, feet marching. Gosling looked after him, then looked up at Delamare and grinned. Delamare grinned back – and then looked up to find everyone else staring at him.

Pursing his mouth, looking sidelong, Delamare said, 'All true. All done by the miracle of electricity.' He looked at Gosling, who had risen to his feet again. 'And very well done, though I say so as shouldn't.'

Gosling nodded, with the hint of a bow. 'Very well done.' Delamare was flattered.

Annie Shepherd broke into loud sobs: her mouth pulled awry in ugly shapes, her eyes screwed up, her face reddening. 'Look what you've done!' Marie Fletcher shrieked, putting her arm round Annie's thick shoulders.

'I'm sorry,' Delamare said politely.

'You dirty rotten liar!'

'You've been making fools of us?' Dean said. It seemed he still hadn't caught on. Delamare felt a slight relief at seeing the door open and the large bulk of Ogden come in.

'Been taking our money and conning us?' Dean said. 'And you!' he said, turning suddenly on Gosling. 'I bet you think you're smart, don't you? I bet you think this is all a good laugh?'

'The bearer of bad news always suffers for it,' Delamare said to Gosling, and Dean's furious glare shifted to him. Red and blustering, Delamare thought, with a tinge of disappointment. There'd been more chance of real violence from Dorking, but he'd chosen to walk out.

'What's going on here?' Ogden asked, with the air of a policeman coming along to break up trouble.

Delamare got up, touched Gosling's arm, and guided him to the back of the dais while, with more bluster, with howls from Annie and invective from Marie, Ogden gathered them together and forced them through the door. The din, the shouts, the rumbling of Ogden's voice, went on in the hall for a long time. Delamare looked steadily at Gosling while it went on, still feeling in control, despite everything. He enjoyed studying the young face, he enjoyed the moments when Gosling's gaze had to slide aside, or when Gosling smiled or raised his straight brows at a particularly shrill or loud cry outside the room.

Ogden came back in, saying, 'Mrs Fletcher's going straight round to the police.'

Delamare laughed.

'Shall I chuck him out now? None too gently?' Ogden nodded towards Gosling.

'Oggie, what are you thinking of? I suggest we adjourn to a more comfortable room.'

Delamare's sitting room was small, its walls filled with books, its armchairs of dark-green leather. The light came from lamps shaded in rose-pink, giving a warm, flattering light which lent Gosling's ivory-pale face a young rosiness. Two of the armchairs were pushed close together. Delamare gestured Gosling into one, and himself took the other.

'Cocoa and biscuits, I think, Oggie.' Ogden, after

giving him one disapproving look, left the room.

Delamare rested his chin on his fist, and leant towards Gosling across the two chair-arms that separated them. He looked steadily into the young man's eyes and smiled.

Gosling sat back in the dark chair, looking small in its embrace. He returned Delamare's gaze, but didn't lean towards him.

'They'll all be back again in a few weeks,' Delamare said. 'Annie will, for certain. "The proofs" mean too much to her. I'll tell them what I've told people before – that I only use electricity when I feel too tired or ill to make genuine contact – I'm just too kind hearted to disappoint them. They'll believe it! Oh,' he admitted, in the face of Gosling's steady, bright stare – and perhaps because of the glimpse of teeth between the lips, 'maybe one or two of them won't come back. But most will. Dorking will. And new members will join. There's a mug born every minute, sweetheart.'

Gosling at last shifted in his seat and leant towards him. Delamare felt a warmth of pleasure. He could see himself in the dark eyes again. The slightly, but charmingly prominent teeth appeared and disappeared as he spoke. 'How can you be so sure?'

'Oh,' Delamare leant just a fraction closer still. 'I've been – er – denounced before, you know.' He smiled. 'I was going to say, "exposed", but I choose my words carefully.'

To his delight, Gosling smiled: that movingly beautiful smile that showed the sharp, narrow arch of his teeth, saddened his eyes and softened his face. And, as with the Cheshire cat, his smile was the last thing to vanish.

Delamare leapt up, as if a spider had dropped on his sleeve.

And then in blundered Ogden, with the cocoa and biscuits.

Ernes Wood

The night was wet, and the road and pavement shone with water, while the yellow light from the shop windows, the red and green from the traffic-lights, the white from the cars' headlights, shimmered and wavered.

The Red Cow was a big pub, a big, handsome, old-fashioned pub of red brick, with a painted sign swinging from a post in its forecourt, and grey, engraved windows which shone brightly through the wet and dark. Noise of music, glasses and shouting tumbled from its open door, and people came and went through it constantly.

To Geoff, leaning against a car on the forecourt, the collar of his jacket turned up, it only mattered that it was his grandad's local. Most nights his grandad was to be found in there. Most nights, at about half-ten, the old man rolled out and started home.

A man, not his grandad, came out of the pub and walked across the forecourt, straight towards him, staring hard at Geoff as he came. Geoff got up from the car. 'Got the time, Mister?' The man was looking at the car where Geoff had been leaning. 'I ain't done it no harm.'

The man unlocked his car, then looked at his watch as he got inside. 'Just after ten.'

'Thanks.' Geoff moved on to another car, and sat on its bonnet. He looked up and down the street. People were walking along in laughing groups, or dashing across the busy road, or waiting at the traffic-lights. Cars went by and went by, dazzling with their rain-starred headlamps. Geoff was worried that, if Peters was in the crowd, he wouldn't spot him in time to be away. It wasn't likely, really, that Peters would come looking for him, but if he did . . . Geoff would have liked to wait somewhere else, somewhere less obvious – and less wet – but then he might miss his grandad. The old man might come out any minute.

Geoff walked up and down the pub's forecourt, keeping his eyes on the pub door. His shoes were letting in water, and his toes were cold. And then he saw his grandad, glimpsed him leaving the pub behind a crowd of other people, but it took only a second for him to recognise the tall, thin figure walking at that hurried slant. Geoff ran back across the forecourt, splashing up to the old man, who reared back in surprise.

'Only me, Grandad.'

His grandad put a hand on his shoulder, leaning heavily on him. 'Hello, old son.'

'Can I come home with you, Grandad?'

The old man nodded, and they walked together away

from the pub. Geoff felt relief, and a great affection for the old man. He felt safe now that he was with his grandad. He felt *right*, normal. Just an ordinary boy with his ordinary grandad, living a normal life.

'Why didn't you come in and find me?'

'Didn't want to.' Peters might have been in the pub. Not very likely, but he might have been.

'He been after you again?'

'Yeah.'

The old man clapped his hand on to Geoff's shoulder and said, 'Bastard.' Geoff grinned. His grandad was on his side.

'If he comes asking after me, will you say you don't know where I am?'

'If he comes asking after you,' said the old man, 'I'll punch his lights out.'

'No,' Geoff said. 'No. Leave him.' It scared him, the thought of his grandad picking a fight with Peters. The old man would get hurt.

'Beats me why your mum married him. Her always seemed to have a good head on her before her met him.'

'Her's a stupid cow!' Geoff burst out. 'Always believes him, never me!'

'Ar, all right, all right,' his grandad said, patting him on the shoulder. 'No need for language like that.'

'But her always does, Grandad, her always does!'

'Ar, all right. What have you had to eat? I think I've got a tin of tuna in. We'll take the short cut. Hang on, while I roll me a fag.'

They had come to the entrance of Ernes Wood Lane, and they stopped there while the old man took his tin and papers from his pocket and made his usual slow, deliberate job of rolling a cigarette. Geoff looked into the darkness of the lane.

They had left the main street and the busy traffic behind. Here they were among waste-ground and factories. Ernes Wood Lane was narrow and without pavements: it was edged by blackened walls. The street-lamps were widely spaced, and some were out. The factories, several of them, were closed and derelict. It was a place that felt bad.

'Wood Lane,' Grandad Whitelocke said, shaking out his match. 'There was a wood here once.'

Geoff could still see it. Bushes waved above the tops of walls. Thickets of stinkweed, nettles and tall foxgloves grew along the junction between walls and tarmac. They shifted in the wind, and made the shadows move. A tangle of dim shadows, melting into darkness, thrown by lampposts, telegraph poles, railings, broken walls, gateposts – it was a wood of shadows.

'You could catch pheasant and hares in these woods, if you knowed how,' Grandad said, as they started into those shadows. 'Good hunting. There was a man went poaching in these woods once.'

'In Ernes Wood?' Geoff asked, just to encourage the story. He let all thought of Peters drop away from him. He was with his grandad, and Grandad was telling a story.

'He wouldn't have gone poaching – they hung you for poaching in them days – he wouldn't have gone except his wife was having a babby, see, and it wasn't easy for her. Her didn't want him to go! But they was hard up, and her hadn't been eating right, and he was worried, worried sick. He wanted the doctor for her – but a doctor had to be paid in them days. You'd have to pay a week's wages for the doctor just to come and look at somebody – and then you had to pay for the medicine. Things am bad now, but it was worse then, and don't let anybody tell you otherwise! Anyway, this bloke – Sam, his name was—'

'Ain't that your name, Grandad? Is this story about you?'

'No, not about me. Sam wanted to go poaching for some pheasants, to get the money for the doctor. "Don't you go," says his wife – her name was Anna. "The keepers'll have you," her says—'

'Keepers?'

'Gamekeepers, her meant. It was their job to stop poor folk catching the pheasants. They'd shoot a

33

poacher, given half a chance. "Think how I'll feel if they send you to jail," Anna says. "Don't you go, Sam, don't go," her begged him.

' "Don't you worry," he says. "I'm no fool; I'll keep clear o' the keepers. I'll go where they don't go. I'll go up to Ernes Wood."

' "Ernes Wood!" Anna says. "Keepers don't need to go there. Nobody goes there – it's haunted!" '

Geoff looked around at the lane they were walking down. Their footsteps echoed back from the brick walls with the flat, muffled sound of a wet evening. The remnants of the haunted wood flickered their branches at gateways, and grew among heaps of old tyres in factory yards.

' "Well, that's stupid talk," Sam says.

' "It's always been haunted," Anna says, "as you very well know. Please don't go, Sam. Don't go."

' "All right," he says. "I won't go."

' "Promise?" her says.

' "Cross me heart and hope to die," he says. "I won't go near the place." '

'Did he mean it?' Geoff asked.

'Not a word. But worrying was bad for her, so he swore up and down he wouldn't go near Ernes Wood. But he never kept his promise. No man would, if his missis needed a doctor – well . . .' Remembering that Geoff's dad was dead, and that Peters was no replacement,

Grandad Whitelocke reached out and patted his shoulder. 'So anyway, on the quiet Sam finds out his old throwing stick that he'd gone poaching with before he was married, and he carried it with him in his pocket. That's a stick carved out of blackthorn and weighted with lead. You go through the woods at night – '

Around them the shadows of Ernes Wood shifted.

' – when the pheasants am roosting, and you knock 'em down with the stick. You can kill hares with 'em an' all, if you're good and lucky. And they don't make any noise to fetch the keepers. Sam used to go through Ernes Wood on his way home from the brick-yard – that's where he worked. He'd creep through the trees really quiet – and that's hard, even if the moon is shining – you bash yourself up on the roots and branches – and he'd find the pheasants snoring in the trees and whack! Down he'd knock 'em and wring their necks. He got a good few, and he took 'em to a friend's house and sold 'em to him – he couldn't take 'em home, or Anna'd find out. He saved some of the money – he hid it behind a loose brick in the fireplace. But he spent a lot of it on buying Anna some good food – milk and cheese and beef . . . Am you getting enough to eat?'

'I'm all right, Grandad. Go on.'

'Well, Sam got enough saved up for the midwife, and he was working on getting enough for the doctor. Night after night – especially at full moon – he'd go up to

Ernes Wood, where the keepers didn't go – and he soon knowed why. There was summat in that wood. He'd hear it, following him through the trees, breaking twigs, moving in the grass . . . Many a time he thought the keepers were on to him, and he lay up like a fox in a covert until he was sure they'd gone – and that made his heart thump. But he never saw a keeper. It don't make you happy when you're lying in a dark wood at night, and you hear something big push through the branches, and there's nothing there . . . Or when you see the moonlight throwing shadows that there's nothing there to make. Sam would never have gone near the place more than once if he'd have had any other way of making the money he needed.

'When Anna was near to having the babby, her mother come to stop. Sam got all the money he'd saved out from behind the loose brick and he give it to her mother, and told her to fetch the doctor right off if he was needed. "Don't you worry about the money," he said. "There'll be the money, if it's needed." And then he went off and fetched the midwife, and when her was on her way, he took himself off to Ernes Wood. 'Cos there was none of the father being present at the birth in them days. Dad was sent off to the pub or anywhere he could be got out of the road. And Sam knowed that if the doctor was fetched, he'd need to catch a few more birds.

'It was a chilly night, and wet – like tonight – and

he got cold. And what was more miserable, he didn't catch anything. He was sitting at the edge of the wood, where it run down into the fields, and hugging hisself and shivering, and wondering whether to go home, when he heard something behind him. Them sounds he'd heard before. Something pushing through the branches, something padding over the old leaves, something breathing and panting . . .

'Sam went crawling back into the wood, slithering over the leaves and lifting up the branches – cold water shot down his neck. He was peering and peering into the trees, but it was all shadows, all moving leaves and branches, and a bit of moonlight here and there. He heard something heavy pounding the ground, and a ring and chink of metal, and he saw – or he thought he saw – a big horse go by with a big rider on its back. A dog seemed to pass right by him, padding the ground and sniffing. It was like a hunt going by – in a wood, in the dark!

'Then he catches sight of the rider again. And at the saddle-bow there's a bulge – the huntsman's catch, fastened to his pommel.

'Well, Sam needed that catch. The huntsman didn't need it, with his horse and his dogs, but Sam did. Even if the doctor hadn't been needed, there was still clothes to buy and good food for Anna. And Sam shouted out, "Master—!" '

Grandad Whitelocke shouted out the word, and it echoed down the lane, bouncing from wall to wall. Geoff jumped, and looked all around. He half expected something to come from one of the gateways, attracted by the sound.

Grandad Whitelocke had stopped, and drew Geoff close to him. 'The huntsman reined in, and turned in his saddle and looked back at Sam. He looked more solid. Sam could see the big black bulk of his horse; and there was a dog a few steps from him, a big, black, shaggy dog. He could see the huntsman's head, black against a patch of sky that was shining through the trees.

' "Please, Master," Sam says. "Give us a share of your game, Master. Give us a share."

'And the huntsman took whatever it was he had slung on his saddle, and he tossed it over to Sam. It landed – thud! – in the mud and the leaves, just out of Sam's reach.

'Then the huntsman rode on, and his dogs followed – and Sam couldn't see 'em any more, but he could hear the sound of their treading and breathing – but you hear that in a wood, sometimes. But even when they'd gone – and maybe they was just shadows and wind sounds – there was still the bundle. Sam crawls over to it and scoops it up. He couldn't tell what it was – it was wrapped in a cloth. So he held it under one arm and slithered down the bank, under the branches, until he come out of Ernes Wood into a field.

'Day was coming on by this time, and it was a lot lighter in the field than it had been in the wood. He starts for his house, and soon he can see pretty well. So he stops by hedge and unwraps the bundle, to see what it was the huntsman had give him. It was a dead babby. And while he was looking at it, it vanished away. It had been a solid little body enough, it's face all blue . . . But then he wasn't holding anything: it was gone, even the cloth it'd been wrapped in. So then Sam starts running, running for all he was worth over the fields and down the lanes until he got home. His wife's mother was waiting for him. "I got some bad news for you," her says.

'And he says, "I know, I know. The babby's dead. The huntsman gave it me – it was his catch." And the poor woman thought he was going mad. Her thought her was going to have to look after him as well as her daughter.'

'That's a horrible story!' Geoff said, and his grandad laughed. 'How did the huntsman get the baby anyway?'

'It was the babby's soul he got. That was *the* Huntsman.'

'But it wasn't fair,' Geoff said. 'Sam was only trying to look after his family.'

'Huntsmen don't care about what they hunt. Cats don't care about mice and birds and their families, do they? But Ernes Wood was right here, on this land. And I'll tell you summat else, an' all. My grandad's grandad was named Sam Whitelocke.'

'It's true, then?'

They'd reached the other end of the lane, and Grandad Whitelocke pointed to another overgrown and chipped street sign. 'As true as this is Ernes Wood Lane.'

In Grandad Whitelocke's small, damp house, they ate tuna fish sandwiches, and drank cocoa, and then the old man went up to bed, and Geoff settled down for the night on the settee, covered with spare blankets and coats.

He didn't sleep much. A busy road went by outside the house, and the unfamiliar noise of traffic kept him awake. And he kept thinking about the story, and about Peters, who would have him again in the next few days, no doubt; and about his mother, and his dad; and the way life just went on and on, and there was no reason to think it would ever get any better. His grandad was old, and wouldn't live for ever.

It was still dark when he got up and left the house. He couldn't sleep, so there was no point in lying there and besides, if he stayed until light there was always the chance that Peters would come looking for him there.

He had nowhere in particular to go, and so he went back to Ernes Wood Lane, and stood at its entrance, looking down its length of broken walls, overgrown yards and shadows. He started to walk down it, for no particular reason, except that it was warmer and less boring to keep moving.

The shadows shifted about him: the shadow of a telegraph pole fell across him. He stepped from it into the shadow of a gate and the flickering shadow of tall weeds, sprouting above a wall. A broken lamppost cast a shadow like a ruined tree.

As he trod further down the lane, the sound of his footsteps changed. From being sharp and clear, the sound of shoes on tarmac echoing from brick, they became muffled, softened – and from his feet there began to rise, not the smell of oil and car fumes, but the rich and rotten scent of years of wet leaves lying on a forest floor. As the smell grew stronger, more impossible to mistake, he stopped and looked about him – and saw the trees gathering about him, gathering out of the shadows, forming themselves out of shadows. The light was no longer the light of widely spaced lampposts, but of moonlight finding its way through many leaves.

He felt only the mildest of surprise. Indeed, as he stood still for the space of perhaps ten heart-beats, he saw the bones of the factory gates, the poles and railings emerge from the trees, and he deliberately blinked and allowed the trees to appear again. This was a choice: he could choose the lane or the wood; and he chose the wood.

When he heard the slow, heavy beat of hooves, he walked towards them, making his way through the roots and thorns, ducking beneath branches. The bulk of the horse loomed out of the dark, the rider high above him. The sharp, warm stink of the horse reached him, and a plume of grey mist blew from its nostrils. Behind it came the dogs, panting, padding, their eyes flashing red.

Geoff stood still and the huntsman passed close by him, without glancing at him. Now Geoff's heart beat hard, but he didn't look for the lane. Instead he looked at the huntsman's saddle-bow, and there he saw the bulge of something hanging. He said, 'Sir?' His voice died in the wet air and the huntsman rode on. 'Sir!'

The horse had passed him, but now it stopped. The dogs were about him. He could feel their hot breath on his legs and hands, but his eyes were on the huntsman, who turned in his saddle, one hand resting on his horse's haunch.

'Sir?' Geoff said, and didn't know himself what he wanted.

The huntsman lifted his hand from the horse's back and held it out to Geoff, a large hand, offered, perhaps, in friendship.

Geoff drew back – and almost as instantly started forward. He put his hand into the huntsman's and felt

strong fingers close about and envelop his. He was lifted
– it was like flying. His foot found a brief resting place
on the huntsman's foot, and then he was on the horse's
back . . .

Followed by the dogs, the horse moved forward, into
the wood; and the wood moved aside and became
gateposts, and telegraph poles, signs and railings and
nettles and shadows.

Davie

Davie was my hero when I was a child. I thought there was no one as wonderful as him.

Our farm was at the back of beyond, so all our maids and farm lads had to live with us, we were so far from anywhere. Oh, they were worked hard. My mother and father worked just as hard, mind you, but it wasn't an easy life. The animals were constant work: feeding them, grooming them, milking them, mucking them out . . . And then there was cheese and butter to be made – and candles, because we made our own candles. And all the meals to be cooked – and the men had to keep all the tools and outbuildings in repair, besides the farmwork. And I did my share! My mother made sure of that. She believed in girls staying close by their mothers and learning how to keep house. I'd scrub the floor, scrub the table, peel potatoes, make pastry, wash dishes, fetch water, fetch eggs, fetch milk – oh, anything she could think of for me to do. And if either of us ever had a spare moment, then she'd teach me to knit, or darn, or make buttonholes.

And that was why I thought Davie was so wonderful – because he didn't have to do any of this, you see. He used to run around the hills all day with his dog – that was the way I saw it. He was the shepherd's son, and his father had trained him to the trade since he was knee-high. By the time he was about twelve, when I first started to moon over him, his father was trusting him to work by himself a lot, because his father was sick by then. He used to boast, 'The best little shepherd there is, my Davie.'

Davie never had to stay indoors, getting chapped hands from scrubbing the table. He never had to fiddle about with buttonholes (I still hate doing buttonholes, even now). He never seemed to take orders from anybody. He'd just whistle his dog, and away he'd go. I knew he looked after the sheep in the hills, but I used to enjoy chasing the sheep about – when I could get away from my mother, that is. I thought Davie must be wonderfully brave and strong, to be able to escape from so much boring work and go off to play with his dog and sheep in the hills. When I grow up, I'll marry Davie, I used to think. We'll both go off into the hills and look after the sheep together. Then I won't have to sew and darn and cook meals and scrub floors.

Davie's father was a long time dying, but he did die in the end, when Davie was about fourteen. That left Davie, and his mother, and eight younger children. Davie's mother earned what she could, but she needed Davie's wage, I can tell you. My dad knew that as well as anybody, and he wasn't the worst of men, my dad. He said it'd save him a lot of trouble looking for another shepherd if Davie would just carry on and fill his father's place. To my mother he said, quiet, 'If he's half as good as his father always reckoned he was, he can manage, and I know something about sheep . . . If I turn him off, what's his mother going to do?'

As it turned out, Davie was as good as his father had always said – and he had my prayers to help him! I really fell in love with him when everybody started taking him for granted as the shepherd. And he was a good-looking lad. I thought then that no boy could properly be called handsome unless he looked like Davie – tall and thin as a grass-blade, with a pointed face pretty as a girl's, a straight nose and blue eyes. Sometimes he'd come to the kitchen door to speak to my mother, and he'd take off his cap. My heart used to turn over in me – underneath his cap his hair was thick, and as bright and fair as – I don't know what. Oh, I do, I do! Bright as gorse blossom. Almost white.

And then he was the head of his family. He can do as he likes, I thought, and I envied him as much as I loved him. I still daydreamed about running off into

47

the hills to live with him, and do as I liked all day long.

But all this time, I hardly spoke to him! Most of the year, we hardly saw Davie at all. Shepherding is solitary. During the summer he spent almost all his time in the hills with the sheep. He brought them down to their pens before winter, and we'd see more of him then, but all his time alone had made him shy and, since he was used to walking, he'd go off to his family rather than come into the kitchen and talk. Then, in spring, there'd be the lambing and, later, the shearing – and then he'd be off into the hills again.

I used to run to the window of the kitchen – where I was held prisoner by my mother – to see Davie striding away with his dogs. My heart used to ache, really ache, to see him go, because I knew it might be weeks before I'd catch a glimpse of him again, but at the same time I used to feel like singing because at least he was free. Oh, I tell you, it was true love.

And I was faithful for years, even though I hardly spoke to him. I used to lie in bed making up the flowery speeches I would use when I told him – one day I was going to tell him – how I felt about him. And then I'd make up what he'd say to me, when he told me that he'd loved me for years too. And then we'd be married, of course, and everything would be perfect. I knew, though, that my mum and dad would have something to say to me marrying a shepherd boy.

I suppose he was about sixteen, and I was about thirteen, when he died. It was spring, and the sheep had been let out of the sheds and they'd gone up into the hills – but the weather started to get bad, you see. So Davie went into the hills after them. But the weather got worse and worse – a blizzard, that snowed us in to the windowsills. Davie froze to death.

Everybody was shocked and touched by his death, even those who hadn't thought so much of him while he'd been alive. But he'd been a part of *their* lives, and he'd been so young. They'd been expecting him to go on being part of their lives for a good many years to come, and it was shocking – well, it was frightening – to know that he was dead and gone, all in a night. And everybody was sorry for his mother, of course, poor woman, to lose her husband and her son. Some people just seem to draw bad luck.

I took his death badly. For years after it I couldn't sleep well. I was afraid to sleep, in case I died in the night. I used to keep myself awake by running songs through my head and telling myself stories. Death is so dreadful, and it was so sad that my young hero should stop short like that, and be buried in a hole, and that the end of him. And I was so sad that I never had told

49

him I loved him, or found out whether he loved me. I still wonder about that, sometimes, old as I am now. I don't suppose, really, he ever took any notice of me. I was just his master's fat little girl, but . . . Oh, it took me years to get over his death.

It wasn't until I was nearly fifteen, though, that I heard of Davie's ghost. I'd gone into service on another farm, to earn myself some money and get out from under my mother's thumb, and another girl there asked me, was it true that our farm was haunted?

'No,' I said. 'What makes you think it is?'

She and the other girls started to giggle, but they managed to tell me that the elder brother of one of them had worked on our farm, and he had told her that the place was haunted.

'By what?' I said.

'By a ghost!'

'I know, a ghost! What kind of ghost?'

There was more giggling, but the story got told in the end. It was well-known, they said, that our farm-yard was haunted by the ghost of a tall, thin boy, who wore a cap on his head and a heavy coat, even in summer, and held a shepherd's crook in his hand. He stood in the yard and stared at the farmhouse. And my father knew all about the ghost, went the story, but got angry when anyone mentioned it.

Well, I was astonished. I'd never heard a word about this while I'd lived at home. But then, my father wasn't the kind of man who would tell anyone about ghosts. Ghost stories were for babies, in his opinion. He'd always said so. And my mother never encouraged any talk of the supernatural because, in a large household, with young children and young maids, people can soon become hysterical.

But, obviously, the ghost was Davie. My feelings were so mixed that I didn't know what they were. The notion that something of Davie still existed – and haunted our yard, stared at our windows – frightened me. Horrified me. Wasn't Davie at peace, then? Wasn't he in heaven? But it appealed to me a little, too; and excited me. What if Davie haunted us for love of me? I couldn't resist that idea, could I? But as soon as I'd thought of it, I was even more frightened than before, because I knew plenty of old stories about dead lovers returning to drag their girls out of the world to join them in the grave.

When I went home on my next visit, I asked my mother about it. 'Now then, Joan,' she said. 'There has been some silly talk, but I don't expect you to add to it.'

'It's just talk then, is it?'

'Just talk,' she said. 'I wouldn't go so far as to say

there's no such things as ghosts, because I don't know – but I do know that in all my life, I've never seen one, nor heard anybody that I'd believe say that they'd seen one. And why should Davie come back and haunt us? He never meant us any harm when he was alive.'

'I was told that Dad had seen him,' I said.

'Well, you was told wrong. Your dad's heard talk of it, same as I have, but he's never seen anything. Some folk'll say anything if they think it makes a good story. You shouldn't believe everything you hear.'

So I left it at that. I can't say I never thought about it again. Sometimes I'd feel sure that my parents spoke the truth and there was nothing uncanny about our dull and dirty old farmyard. At other times, when I'd just heard some other version of our haunting told, I'd feel a tremor . . . Once I even spent hours watching from a window for some sign of the ghost to appear. I saw nothing, of course. But I did watch in summer, and the tale-tellers said that the ghost was more often seen in the darkness of winter and early spring.

But time went on and I grew older. I changed my mind a good deal about what makes a man handsome, and my husband, when I married him, was a big strapping lad, with darkish, reddish hair, all over his chest and arms as well as his head: a big burly lad, as hot as a stove. We hadn't anywhere to live, so we moved in with my parents on the old farm again. My mum and dad were glad of the extra help by that time. I suppose I was twenty then, and we've lived here on the farm ever since.

Well, me and Bill – that's my husband, Bill – well, of course we've had rows and fights, but I've never had any real reason to wish for somebody else. And I came to be glad that my mother had made me learn to do all those boring jobs, even if they still bore me. But I never forgot Davie. Oh no. Something would remind me of him – oh, ever so often. The yard that he was supposed to haunt, the sheep, the dogs – even just seeing some lad with very fair hair would remind me of him, and I'd smile at remembering the way I used to hanker after him. Yet, just the same, I'd often cross the yard a dozen times, or help in the shearing, without ever thinking of Davie once.

But when I did think of him, I found that he had quite changed in my memory, especially after my own sons were born. I could remember him quite clearly, but I didn't think of him as the wild free hero any more. I found myself thinking, he was only a child. I looked at my own sons and remembered Davie's pretty, pointed beardless face, and his skinny body and thought: poor boy, poor little boy. To have so much loaded on those thin, bony little shoulders. His mother and all those brothers and sisters, and all the responsibility of the flock. My heart would ache for him then, not after him.

Poor little boy. Such a hard life, and such a short one. All over at sixteen, before his brothers and sisters were old enough to take the load off him. If he'd lived, his life might have turned out a happy one in the end. But that spring storm ended it. I told my own children about him, and I suppose my eldest, William, was about ten when he told me about the ghost in the yard. He asked me, was it Davie's ghost?

My mother told him to be quiet, but I drew him out. Lots of people had seen the boy, William told me. He hadn't himself, and nor had any of his friends, but their older brothers and sisters had, some of them. And friends of theirs had. A boy, with fair hair, wearing a cap, stood in our yard and looked at the house. He carried a shepherd's crook, and he just stood there, staring, but if you went towards him, he disappeared.

Exactly the same story that I'd heard when I was fifteen, though I was twice that age then. The story hadn't changed, and I hadn't seen a thing myself. I asked Bill about the ghost, and yes, he'd heard about it, but no, he hadn't seen it. 'People see him in the winter, mostly,' he said. 'Lit up by the light from our windows.'

'Do you believe there really is something?' I asked him.

My father would have said no straight away. Bill took a long time about answering. 'I've never seen anything myself,' he said. 'But . . . I've felt a bit – odd – sometimes, coming across that yard in the dark.'

'Oh, that's because you've heard about the ghost and you're scared,' I said.

'As likely as not. I don't much like talk about ghosts.'

Well, we get older, don't we? I didn't notice time passing much myself, I was too busy – but soon my eldest was twenty, not ten, and then my dad and mother died within a year of each other. That hit me hard, that grieved me, but I don't mean any disrespect to them when I say that I think I took Davie's death harder. I mean, I was over forty when mum and dad died, and I knew they were going to die; I was braced for it, you might say. But Davie's death was the first death I really noticed, and it was the death of somebody my own age, out of the blue. My mum and dad's deaths, and the funerals made me think a lot of Davie again – I thought of him, and of them, almost every time I stepped into the yard, especially when the winter came and it was cold and dark. I never saw anything, I never heard anything, but I kept thinking of my mum and dad, gone into the cold and dark, and I kept thinking of Davie's death – that poor little boy, all alone in the hills, and getting colder and colder and nobody to help him. Many's the time I stood in the yard and cried for him – or for my mum and dad, but it always seemed to be him I was thinking of. I kept thinking of how scared he must have been when he'd realised that he wasn't going to get home through the snow. Of how he must have grown colder and colder and known he was dying – he would have known that people died of the cold. That was what I couldn't get out of my mind: the terrible loneliness and fear he must have died with.

Bill said that it wouldn't have been like that. He said that as death came closer, Davie would have drifted off into a dream and probably died quite happy. Bill was very good to me at that time, and I wished I could have believed what he said, but I couldn't.

I never saw Davie standing in the yard, as so many people said he did, but it was as if I was haunted just the same. Every time I stepped into the yard, I thought of him. If ever I was working at the sink and looking into the yard, I couldn't stop thinking of him standing out there, looking at the lit windows of the house – that's what people said he did. That poor lonely little boy, who'd spent most of his life alone with the sheep in the hills, who'd died alone in the hills – and came after death to stand in the yard and look at our lit windows. I remembered, so clearly, seeing him walk out of our yard one day, and look back. At the time I'd envied him so much that I'd thought the expression on his face had been one of triumph and gladness: see what freedom I have while you're cooped up in the house peeling potatoes! But now, remembering that look, I saw loneliness and sorrow in a child's face: a child that had longed to be kept indoors and fussed over, and never had been. I'd start crying into the sink: I couldn't bear it. I'd lie awake at night thinking about poor Davie's short, lonely little life, and I'd start crying and wake Bill. He wanted to ask the vicar to come and speak to me. He got very worried about me, Bill did. He was a very good man. I made a good choice when I chose him.

But I didn't need the vicar. I exorcised my ghost myself, and I didn't use bell, book and candle, and I didn't send him packing to the Red Sea either!

What I did was, I set the table. I set the table for me and Bill, and our son and daughter who were still at home, and then I set an extra place. Knife and fork and spoon and plate and everything. And when everybody was seated, I went and opened the kitchen door and I said, aloud, 'Davie – come in love, and get your dinner. You've stood out there long enough!'

Well, the family looked at me a bit odd, but Bill looked at the others under his brows (I saw him) and they didn't say anything. I stood waiting at the kitchen door, waited for more than long enough for somebody to cross the yard and come in, and then I shut the door and went to the table. I served everybody, and I put a helping on the plate in front of the empty chair, and said, 'Eat up, Davie!' I passed him the salt and made sure he had a helping of pudding too, when everybody else had cleared their plates.

'He shouldn't have pudding, mum,' my daughter said. 'He hasn't eaten his firsts!'

'Davie's a guest,' I said. 'He can do what he likes.'

When we'd finished, I set a little stool right by the warm fire and said, 'Davie, come to the fire and warm yourself, my love. That's your place for as long as you want it.'

And whenever I started brooding about his death after that, I'd open the kitchen door and say, 'Get in here Davie, and stop moithering me.' And it always made me feel better. After a bit I stopped feeling so bad about it, and I haven't heard that story about Davie standing in the yard staring at our windows for – oh, for ever so long.

Do I think he's in the house? Yes, I do. I've never seen him, nor ever heard that anybody else has, and I've never heard anything, but I think he's in here, yes. The house is more companionable now than it used to be. You know how you can walk into a house and know that there's somebody in the house, even if they're up in a back bedroom and you can't see or hear them? And sometimes, you go into a house, and you know it's empty, and you're going to have to go out into the yard to find somebody. There's something about the air in a house that changes when there's somebody in it.

Well, this house is never empty now. Even when I come in from the yard, and I know everybody else is out – there's still something in the air that tells me somebody's home. I often talk to him. I never get any answer, but I don't mind that. I wish I could do more for him, my poor Davie. I'd like to give him a present this Christmas, but to give a present is a sure way to lay a ghost and the truth is, I don't want to lose my Davie a second time.

Gene Genie

Physical Appearance.

The clients expressed a preference for a fair-haired, blue eyed boy. This was easily achieved, the parents being of Caucasian northern stock. The eyes will be a true blue, not grey; but the hair a light brown rather than a true blond. With the genes available it was impossible to achieve a lighter hair tone without the hair appearing ginger, which the clients had expressly requested should not be the case. The clients accept this.

After viewing the possible adult faces, the clients chose face 1b (see attached sheet).

Owing to unfortunate gene linkings, it has proved impossible to achieve the above appearance without also accepting large, prominent ears. The clients have agreed to this, as the ears can always be surgically corrected once the child is born.

The child, provided it is given adequate nourishment (see appendix 1) will achieve an adult height of between 5' 11" and 6' 1", which the clients find acceptable.

The child will have no undue propensity for weight gain. However, it has been stressed to the clients, and they accept, that weight gain is more a matter of nurture than genetics. The clients accept that Gene Genie will accept no responsibility for baby Bobrick's overweight at any time after birth, even gross obesity.

Longevity.

Accidents excepted, and provided a healthy lifestyle is followed, baby Bobrick should enjoy a life of at least seventy years or longer. It should be emphasised, however, that strong genes, though off-setting the effects of an unhealthy lifestyle, cannot altogether overcome it. An inherited tendency towards a weak chest indicates that baby Bobrick should avoid smoking in particular.

Talents.

The clients expressed a wish that the child should be musically gifted. It has been explained to them, and they accept, that such talent is not entirely genetically determined, and no absolute guarantee can be given.

However, our engineers have succeeded in ensuring that the child will have superior patterning skills, manual dexterity and a good ear.

If the appropriate programme of encouragement, exposure and reward is followed (see appendix 3) there is a more than seventy per cent chance that baby Bobrick will become musically talented.

If not, then his genetic programming should make the acquirement of other skills an easy matter.

An IQ of above 135 is guaranteed. It cannot be guaranteed, of course, that baby Bobrick will be a high achiever. That is a matter of nurture. The clients may wish to attend counselling sessions on how to ensure their child achieves.

Personality.
The clients accept that personality is multi-factored, owing much to nurture: also that most genetic influences in this area are still being unravelled. However, our engineers can assure the clients that baby Bobrick's personality will tend towards the dominant, leader-type, and will have a reasonable stability.

The clients understand that nurture can entirely overset the influence of genetics on personality, as far as can be estimated with our present state of knowledge. They have, therefore, been counselled to seek guidance in child-rearing principles, and to attend frequent refresher courses during the child's development.

Edgeware read through the document carefully, keeping it pinned in place on his desk with a forefinger at the corners of the bottom edge. Having taken in – he hoped – all the details, he raised his eyes. Three people sat on the soft chairs grouped beside, not in front of, his desk. He had been careful to arrange the furniture in his office so that it was impossible to take up a confrontational position without putting a great deal of effort into dragging heavy chairs about.

The lawyer was professionally calm and controlled, dressed in a smart, dark suit and gold-rimmed spectacles, her dark hair cropped short. She held a note-pad and a gold pen against her knee.

The Bobricks sat with their knees crossed and their hands clasped in their laps, echoing each other. They were both in their fifties, with well-kept hair, his darkened to hide the grey, hers left with grey highlights. Everything they wore – their shoes, their watches, his light-grey suit, her navy-blue coat-dress, her ring and necklace – were plain and expensive. Together they presented an image: a rich, close, tasteful couple. Edgeware kept his face still, and hoped that the faint contempt he had come to feel for all his company's clients didn't show.

'I don't see the problem,' Edgeware said.

'Shall I—?' the lawyer asked, shifting in her seat and turning slightly towards her clients.

Mrs Bobrick interrupted, her voice low-pitched and surprisingly pleasing, even seductive. Vocal training, Edgeware thought. He'd paid for some himself, to increase his career chances. 'We were going to have only one child,' she said. 'It seemed to make good sense to invest in the best possible child we could have.'

Edgeware flexed his fingers slightly above the document. 'Our engineers have managed that, I think.'

Mrs Bobrick nodded glumly. Her husband said,

'Laurence was a wonderful son. All we could have wished.'

A little shiver of awareness went through Edgeware. 'Was?'

The lawyer, after a glance at her clients, tapped her paper with the gold pen, reminding Edgeware of a teacher wishing to recall his attention. 'Laurence Bobrick is dead.'

'He wasn't twenty,' Mrs Bobrick added. A ripple seemed to move through the muscles of her face, but passed, and left her calm.

'Ah.' Edgeware pushed himself away from his desk, leant back in his chair, already feeling the thrill of winning. No way were they going to get anywhere with this. 'The company can accept no responsibility—'

'There was no accident involved,' said the lawyer. 'And Laurence had regular medical check-ups, and can be shown to have been an extremely fit, healthy young man. But he lived only twenty years instead of the life of "at least seventy years" promised by Gene Genie, "accidents excepted and provided a healthy lifestyle is followed". There'll be no difficulty in demonstrating that it was. Life-long.' She turned her head to look at her clients. 'Mr and Mrs Bobrick have been exemplary, extremely responsible parents.'

Protecting their investment, Edgeware thought.

Mr Bobrick said, 'Laurence played tennis.'

Edgeware sat still and quiet, and clasped his own hands as he thought through what he might say, and what their answers might be. 'I'm extremely sorry for your loss,' he remembered to say, 'but can I ask, if it isn't too intrusive a question – if it wasn't an accident and your son was in perfect health . . . ?'

Mrs Bobrick said, 'He slashed open his own face and then his throat.'

'Ah. Suicide.'

'Suicide,' said the lawyer, and, looking at the document on Edgeware's desk, raised her brows. She tapped the pad on her knee. There was no mention, she conveyed, of suicide in the document. True enough, this gene reading had been done in the early, wing-and-prayer days of Gene Genie's operations, when the company had been run by creative scientists who worked more for the joy of it than for money, and rushed into frighteningly careless agreements, just for the chance of playing about with genes. Increasingly, these early deals were coming back to haunt Edgeware and Gene Genie's legal staff.

'Are you – I hope this won't sound callous, but are you sure that it was suicide?'

'Are you suggesting,' the lawyer asked, 'that Laurence Bobrick was murdered?'

'It was suicide,' Mrs Bobrick said. 'It is quite certain.'

'I see.' Edgeware leant forward in his chair again

and folded his arms on his desk. 'And what do you hope for from Gene Genie?'

The lawyer tapped her pen on her pad again, in that irritating way. 'To begin with, acknowledgement of your responsibility.'

'I'm sorry, but I don't see how we can be held responsible.' How much does she know? Edgeware thought.

The lawyer's expression was perfectly blank. 'You promised my clients a "reasonable stability" of mind.'

'Of *personality.*'

'Arguably, it comes to the same thing. But can someone who commits suicide be said to be stable?'

'Arguably, yes,' Edgeware said.

'Shall we argue it in court?'

Edgeware felt a chill in his belly. The lawyer did know . . .

'We haven't yet discussed the reason *why* Laurence Bobrick committed suicide,' the lawyer continued.

She did know . . . Edgeware raised his brows questioningly, as if he had no idea of the reason, but would be interested to hear it.

The lawyer pointed, with her pen, towards Edgeware's desk. 'The suicide note was that document. Clipped to it was a sheet of paper on which Laurence had written, "Because of this". Then he slashed his face open diagonally, and—' She politely broke off as Mrs Bobrick interrupted.

'He didn't know,' she said. 'We'd never told him we'd had a gene reading – why should it ever come up? I don't know what he was looking for when he found it.'

The lawyer leant forward and said eagerly, 'Imagine the effect on a sensitive young man – a good-looking, highly intelligent young man, a talented musician, hoping to make music his career – who imagines all these advantages to be gifts from the gods. And then he discovers this report – realises that no, his whole life has, in fact, been planned – that *he* has been planned. His talent, his intelligence – even the very face he sees in the mirror – he realises that none of these things are really his, none of them his creation. No. They've all been chosen, bought and paid for by his parents, rather as they choose the decor of their house!'

Edgeware saw the Bobricks flinch. If the lawyer noticed, she didn't care.

With a feeling of panic that seemed to rise through the seat of his chair upwards, Edgeware said, 'Gene Genie can hardly be held responsible for Laurence Bobrick finding a paper that should have been in the bank.' He smiled. 'I think that might come under "act of God".'

'Perhaps. But Laurence is not an isolated case, is he, Mr Edgeware?'

Oh God. She did know.

'If you force us to go to court,' the lawyer went on, 'if we have to seek out all the other similar cases – if all this goes public, imagine . . . "If you've had a gene reading, don't, whatever you do, ever let the knowledge of it slip out to your child . . ."'

Edgeware covered his mouth with one hand and held it there while he returned the lawyer's pointed gaze. Her eyes, large and brown, stared straight back into his without shifting or even blinking. Finally he shifted the hand slightly and asked, 'What do you want?'

With a soft shifting of her beautifully styled hair, Mrs Bobrick raised her lowered head and gave him one look. Without anything more being said, Edgeware knew what she wanted.

A week later, they all met again. 'It's good news – let's sit in my cosy corner,' Edgeware said, ushering them to the corner of his office, where soft leather seats were grouped round a low marble-topped table. A bone china pot of hot coffee was already waiting, and Edgeware poured coffee for everyone.

'I'm sorry to have kept you waiting,' he said, 'but I'm sure you realise that I don't have the authority to give the go-ahead on something as expensive as this. There have been *very* high-level talks on this, I can promise you.'

The lawyer and the Bobricks smiled politely. Mrs

Bobrick, sensing that she was going to get her way, murmured, 'Of course, we understand.'

Edgeware lifted a sheaf of documents which lay waiting on the leather seat beside him, and shuffled them together against his knee. 'Mrs Bobrick, you realise that you'll have to undergo extensive hormone management?'

'Of course,' she repeated, with one of her graceful nods, her hair shifting out of place and back again. 'My age . . .'

'Yes.' Edgeware coughed, and handed her the papers. 'Well, we shall need your signature on these waiver forms, relieving us of all responsibility for any, er—'

'Side-effects,' said the lawyer. 'Mrs Bobrick, you know—'

'I'll sign,' she said, waving a hand. The nails were manicured, but uncoloured. 'Julian, do you have a pen?' Her husband took a silver pen from his breast-pocket and handed it to her. Everyone watched as she methodically went through the papers, signing.

'Well!' said Edgeware, when she handed the papers back to him. 'I'll start everything moving as quickly as possible. We're delighted, Mrs Bobrick – Mr Bobrick – to be recreating Laurence for you. Invite me to the christening, won't you?'

They laughed, and all shook hands.

The Landing Window

The Portway is a steep hill. For most of its stretch there are no pavements, and there are signs in the hedges, half overgrown by hawthorns and hazels, warning traffic of just how steep it is. The Portway – the way along which goods are portered, or carried – is a very old name. Stone-age people, I've been told, carried salt over it, but I can't say how true that is.

Climb The Portway from the Hadley side, and you climb panting through an estate of new, neat little houses, all built of neat, new pale-orange bricks with dainty stripes of pale mortar between them. Their paint is still clean and bright, and they all have big windows with vases of flowers placed in the centre and frilly curtains on either side. A smooth, mown lawn in front of every house, with beds of flowers planted round the edges, and a great many of the doors have hanging baskets of flowers in the porches. In every drive there's a clean car parked on tidy gravel. And trees, there are trees everywhere along this street: one or two big wild elms and chestnuts, from the time before the houses were built, but mostly little flowering cherries, lilacs and laburnums.

Then you get to the top of the hill and the neat, nice, new estate stops. You come to rows of concrete posts, broken to show the pebbles at their centres. Between them sags diamond-meshed wire, jacketed in rust. Behind that fence everything's gone wild. There are so many dandelions that, when they've all run to seed, the fields look as if they're covered with cobweb. The grass grows nearly to your shoulders, and the buttercups and campion grow tall and straggly, to reach the light. It's a struggle even to walk past the fence, because the hawthorns grow through the wire mesh and hang over it and the road. There is no pavement once you're past the new estate, and you have a choice between walking in the middle of the road, or getting your face scratched to pieces by the hawthorns. These wild, overgrown fields, on both sides of the road, are all that's left of Dancers Farm. There used to be a lot more land, but Mick sold most of it to the builders who built that new estate.

Dancers farmhouse stands close to the road, a little below the top of the hill. It's nothing like the houses round it. They're ten years old, maybe: Dancers is four hundred. In the wooden beam over the door is carved the date 1567.

Dancers looks every year of its age. The roof's covered with dark, blue-black tiles, and grown all over with blotches of yellow and orange lichen, and big cushions of long, bright-green moss. It even has some tufts of grass and flowers growing on the roof, where soil and seeds have lodged in cracks. The whole roof ripples up and down – up where the tiles go over the wooden roof beams, and down where there are no beams and the tiles are collapsing. The roof's holed too, at one end: the rain falls in the bedroom where Mick's mum and dad used to sleep.

It's no use knocking at Dancers' front door, because Mick won't hear, and the door won't open anyway. You have to go round the back and in by the kitchen door. It opens into a low passage that smells thickly and warmly of old cooking, old newspapers, and old tobacco smoke. Just inside the door a flight of narrow, steep stairs, made of old, worn, black wood, lead up to the first floor. There's a landing half-way up, in the corner of the stairs, and a little landing window lets a smudge of light into the fuggy dimness.

Dancers' windows are all tiny, and the door's so small that even I have to duck, and I'm not tall. Inside the ceilings are low, and when I'm in there I always walk about with my hand on top of my head, because I've banged my head on the roof beams and door-lintels so often. The floorboards are always tripping you up too, because they've twisted and risen. It's a wonderful house to visit, but not, I think, to live in. The rooms

73

are small and badly lit, and at night most of the house is in pitch-darkness because there's no electricity. Mick never got around to having electricity put in.

'I got me oil-lamp in the kitchen,' he says. 'I can read by that if I want to. And me little radio runs on batteries. And I've gone to bed in the dark all me life. I'm used to it. So I never got round to the 'lectric. Don't think I'll bother now.'

At the back of Dancers is an untidy yard. Piled up seed boxes have slithered down in avalanches; broken flowerpots and broken tools have been thrown in amongst them and on top of them. There are piles of old newspapers, swelling and softening in the rain, and hamburger boxes and plastic rubbish bags. Weeds have grown up through all of it, long, thin, unhealthy weeds. There's a path through all of this rubbish to the old pigsty.

There's nothing in the pigsty except more rubbish now; Mick stopped keeping pigs years ago. But he likes to go out and sit on the pigsty wall because there's a wonderful view of the valley below the farm. You can see the whole district for miles around: roads, television masts, canals, cooling-towers, factories, houses, railways, flats, parks, power-stations. It looks best at night, when it's all lit up. Then the blocks of flats are towers of lights, like the masts of giant ships sailing by. The little roads are marked out by double strings of white lights, and the main roads by double strings of orange ones. The towers of floodlights shine white from the football grounds; the television masts are topped by red lights; and aeroplanes circling for Birmingham airport flash red and green. And below them, all the hundreds – thousands – of shops and houses have lights in their windows. There are so many lights that they make a haze in the sky, lighting up the darkness. Mick often goes into his yard at night, just to look at the lights. 'Better than Blackpool illuminations,' he says. 'Like basketfuls of jewels on a black velvet cloth.'

'There wasn't all them lights when I was a little lad,' Mick told me once. 'Nor so many factories and houses. And we didn't have all these houses next door. Dancers was out in the wilds then. All this hill was fields and rough ground. No other houses for miles.'

We were sitting on the pigsty wall, drinking mugs of tea, and it was almost dark.

'Why's it called Dancers, Mick?' I asked.

Mick took a long drink from his mug, as if he was thinking; then he said,

'Me and Lou used to walk near two miles to school every day, and we was only little uns. We'd go down these fields here – well, they was fields then – and through a little wood that used to be there. It was like a jungle to us, that wood. We'd go across a stream, and then on to that road down there at the bottom of the hill, and across the railway lines and past the factory gates. It was a long way to walk twice a day and we had work to do when we got home at night – feeding animals and dusting and polishing in the house. You young uns have it easy.'

'Lou was your sister?' I said.

'Me big sister. Ar. It's been a good few years since her died. Tuberculosis, that's what killed her, when her was just a young woman. A lot of folk died of tuberculosis then. But when we was little, her used to hold my hand when we went up to bed.'

' 'Cos you were scared of the dark?'

'Scared?' Mick said. 'I was terrified. It's such an old house, Dancers. I'd heard me mother say that her grandad had died in the room where her and me dad slept. And that started me thinking about how many folk had lived here in all them hundreds of years, and how a lot of 'em must have died here, and I never stopped thinking about ghosts. Our mother used to say, 'Bed!' and we'd have to go off to bed by ourselves, in the dark. Along that passage and up them stairs in the pitch-black. Mother wouldn't come with us, nor give we a candle or a lamp in case we started a fire. Well, it wasn't so bad in the summer, but you know yourself that on a winter's night, you can't see your hand in front of your face in them passages.'

'I'm always falling over the floorboards,' I said.

76

'Well, I would never have gone to bed if it hadn't been for Lou. I think her was as scared as I was, but her never would admit it. Her'd grab my hand and off her'd march down that dark passage, singing,

"He who would valiant be, let him come hither,"

and squeezing me fingers together into a lump. I'd hang on to her jumper with me other hand, to keep right close behind her. I was too scared to sing. I used to think the ghosts would come after me if I made a noise they could hear, but Lou thought singing a hymn would keep 'em away, and her must have been right, because no ghosts ever did come after we. When we got to the stairs, her'd stop a minute, and sing out, really loud,

"Hobgoblins nor foul fiends shall daunt his spirit!

"He knows he at the end shall life inherit!"

I think her was more scared of the stairs than of anywhere else. I think her was telling any hobgoblins or foul fiends that might be hanging about on them stairs to get out of the way. Up we'd go, Lou in front, feeling the way and singing, and me snivelling behind. And you know that little landing on the stairs, half-way up?'

'I know it,' I said.

'And the little window there? We'd always stop on that landing, because of that window. It was always lighter there, especially if the moon was shining, and we felt safer. Lou would always take a look out of that window, and sometimes her'd lift me up, so I could

77

look through it an' all . . .' Mick stopped and had a think about something. 'You want to know why the farm's called Dancers?' he asked.

'I was wondering,' I said.

I thought he was going to tell me, but he said, 'Well, I don't know. Anyroad, after we'd had a look through the window, we'd go on up the rest of the stairs, and Lou'd start singing again.

"Those who beset him round with dismal stories,

"Do but themselves confound, his strength the more is!"

My favourite hymn, that. We'd get to our room, and Lou'd see me tucked up afore her went to her own bed. And then her'd tell me stories to keep me mind off ghosts until I fell asleep.'

'Who told *her* stories to keep *her* mind off ghosts?'

'Nobody,' Mick said. 'Poor old Lou. Poor frightened little wench.'

'Brave little wench!' I said.

'Ar, brave. Her looked after me, did our Lou. Our mum and dad didn't mean to be cruel, mind. That was just the way folk brought up children in them days. No fussing.'

'Are you still scared of the dark?' I asked.

'I still sing "He who would valiant be," on me way up to bed sometimes, but not to keep ghosts away. Ghosts! I stopped being scared of them a long time ago. But if I had any children, I wouldn't make 'em go up to bed on their own in the dark.' He stopped talking and sat and looked at the valley. It was full dark now, and the lights shone and shone for miles, orange and white, and red and blue and green, glittering below us. 'I still stop and look out the landing window,' Mick said.

'That's on the other side of the house, isn't it?' I said. 'It doesn't look out on these lights.'

'No. Nothing so cheerful. You can see over the hedge and into the fields on the other side of the road. You can see that little hill . . . Me dad'd have a fit if he could see the state them fields am in.'

'You mean the little hill with the hawthorns growing on it? I walk over there sometimes – 'specially when the hawthorns are in flower.'

'I'd never sell that land,' Mick said, and became thoughtful. After a long silence, he asked, 'Why do you think the place is called Dancers?'

'I dunno. I suppose somebody called Dancer owned it once.'

'My family have owned it for as long back as anybody knows,' Mick said. His family was named Worley.

'Then maybe it's a word being said wrongly. You know, like The Elephant and Castle should really be L'Infanta De Castile.'

'Could be,' Mick said.

'Mick – do you *know* why it's called Dancers?'

'Let's go in now,' Mick said. 'It's getting cold.'

We went into Dancers' kitchen, where the reeking oil-lamp hung from a hook in the ceiling, lit and hissing, casting a dingy yellow light on things close by, but hardly lighting the corners at all. It was a big, shadowy room. Mick thought it was comfortable. He had an old armchair by the fire, and a grubby little stool to put his feet on. Visitors had to sit on straight-backed chairs at a table covered with newspapers instead of a cloth.

I took my jacket from the back of a chair and was going to say goodbye, and leave, but Mick said, 'No, stop. I'll make some more tea. And I'll tell you something I've not told anyone else, ever.'

Well, I had to stay to hear that.

'I growed up on this farm,' Mick said, as he put the kettle on. 'I didn't have to go looking for a job: there was too much work to be done here. And then Lou died when her was about nineteen: I told you that. I hadn't been worried about ghosts for a long time, but it hit me hard when her died. Me only sister, you know: I missed her a lot. Then there was just me, mum and dad, and it was like that for a long time. We sold some of the fields when Dad was getting old and there was too much land for we to manage. We sold a bit more when Dad died; and me and Mum tried to keep things going, but it was too much for we, so we sold nearly all the land and the animals, and just kept some pigs and hens, to feed weselves. Growed some vegetables, kept a cow – we did all right. These new houses was going up all round us, though.

'Then Mum died, and I was on me own, and I was pretty miserable. Bored. Lonely. Used to go down the hill there, to the pub. Used to go for the company, but I'd come back tiddly, singing, "He who would valiant be, let him come hither," all the way back up the hill. And this one night I'm going to tell you about, I come in more drunk than usual. I was going down the passage to the stairs, and I was falling from one side to the other in the pitch-dark, singing at the top of me voice. I clambered up the stairs, on all fours most of the way, and I got to the landing. The moon was shining through the window. Beautiful, it was. Everywhere the moon shone was white, and the shadows were black. And I thought, "I'll look out the window, like Lou used to do . ! ." Because I hadn't bothered to look through that window for years – not since I'd got too big to admit I was scared of the dark and had started going to bed on me own. I'd got into the habit of going straight past the window without bothering to look. But this night, I looked. I stopped singing, and I just stood there and looked through that window. What do you think I saw?'

'I don't know, Mick,' I said. 'I've no idea at all.'

The kettle was boiling, and Mick got up and poured boiling water into the teapot slowly and carefully. I got impatient and said, 'What did you see, Mick?'

'I saw what I used to see when Lou lifted me up to look through that window when I was a little lad.' He brought the teapot to the table.

'Tell me, Mick!' I said.

'Dancers,' he said. 'I saw dancers. I saw the fields across the road, all grey in the moonlight, and the trees and bushes all black – and something was moving on the hill. I stared hard, and it was people – people dancing in a ring. No music. I couldn't hear nothing, being behind glass, in the house, but I could tell they was dancing. And I remembered then – that's what Lou used to show me. That was what her used to look for every night. Them dancers.'

'Who were they?'

'Ah,' he said. 'That's a good question: who was they?'

'Didn't you ever ask your mum and dad about them? I mean, when you were little and you used to see them?'

'I never mentioned 'em to anybody. Nor did Lou. I don't think we even talked about 'em to each other. No point. Nothing to say about 'em . . . And by the time I'd growed up, I'd forgot about 'em. I had other things to think about. It wasn't until I come home drunk that night and stopped to look out the window that I remembered. And I stood there and remembered all the dozens and dozens of times I'd seen them dancing when I was a little boy – and here I was a full-grown man, and they was still dancing. I wondered if I'd dreamed seeing them when I was little, or if I was dreaming then – or was the dancers dreaming *me* and I wasn't really there.'

'You're making me feel dizzy,' I said.

'How do you think I felt? I was drunk! And then I thought maybe the dancers was real, and trespassing on my land. Well, you read about these witches in the papers, don't you? Prancing round in the nuddy – well, not on my land, you don't, I thought. I went out to ask 'em what they thought they was doing. Back down the stairs I went – nearly fell down 'em – and out of the house and across the road – nearly got knocked down. I went through that little gap in the hedge and into the field, and I could see the dancers then, dancing ring-a-ring-a-roses on the side of the hill. But I still couldn't hear any music, or any sound from them at all. I could only hear noises from the new houses – cars, and voices shouting goodnight – but the closer I went to the dancers, the quieter them noises got. They faded away very quick, quicker than they should have done. It was as if I was miles from anywhere, when I'd only come a few steps from the road. And *then* I heard the dancers' music.'

'What was it like?'

Mick shook his head. 'I don't know a lot about music. I couldn't say. It was quick, you know, lively – and sad. Lively, but sad . . . And the dancers . . . There was men and women dressed in all sorts of clothes, some like I'd never seen. Round and round they went in a big circle – and one of the women looked over her shoulder at me. It was Lou.'

'Your sister.'

'Lou, me sister. I knowed her straight away. I hadn't seen her for so many years, and her was older than the photos I had of her. It was Lou though.'

'But she was dead,' I said.

'I know her was! I went to her funeral. But her was there, going round and round in the dance and looking happy and healthy enough.'

'You were dreaming,' I said.

'You think so? I just stood there, watching. There was music playing, but I couldn't see anybody playing it. I kept thinking that either me or the dancers wasn't real, and I didn't want to find out which it was. Every time Lou went past, her'd look at me, and smile. And then her let go of the dancer next to her and held out her hand to me.'

I took a quick breath. 'Did you take her hand?'

'I wanted to. I was going to. But just afore our skins touched, I said, "Lou—?" I meant to say, "Lou, are you

84

alive?" but all I got the chance to say was, "Lou—?" And as soon as I made that sound, everything went away. Lou went away. All the dancers did. They just went. The music stopped – like a radio had been switched off. It was dark and quiet. I was standing in a field, drunk, in the dark, and there was a cold breeze blowing in me face. No music, no dancers – I could hear cars passing on the road, loud as we can hear them now.'

'You were drunk,' I said. 'You were dreaming.'

'I was in the field, not in me bed.'

'You were sleepwalking.'

'I was fully-dressed,' he said. 'I hadn't got out of bed and walked in me sleep.'

'Maybe you'd gone to bed in your clothes,' I said.

'Maybe. But then, what about all the times I'd seen the dancers when I was little, when Lou lifted me up to the window? And what I keep wondering is – what did Lou see when her looked through the window? Her always did. Long after I stopped, when I was a big lad of sixteen or so, I'd see her looking out of that window late at night. What did her see? Did her see herself, dancing, out there? That's what I want to know. Do you think her did?'

'I think this is what happened,' I said. 'You came home drunk and went to bed in your clothes. You dreamed about when you were a little boy, and you dreamed about you and Lou seeing the dancers. Then you started walking in your sleep, and you walked out to the field. You dreamed you saw Lou with the dancers. Then you woke up and found yourself in the field. See? It's simple.'

'If that's true,' Mick said, 'then why is the farm called Dancers if there are no dancers?'

'It's *because* the farm's called Dancers that you dreamed about dancers,' I said. 'If the farm had been called The Elephant and Castle, you'd have dreamed of Lou riding an elephant in a castle.'

Mick sat and thought about that while he drank his tea. Then he smiled and shook his head. 'You come with me,' he said, and went out of the kitchen, beckoning me to follow.

We left the lamp in the kitchen, and it was so dark in the passage that I couldn't see anything at all. I put my hand on top of my head, so I wouldn't bang it on the beams, but then nearly fell, tripping on a floorboard. 'Mick?' I said. I could hear him coming back towards me – at least, I hoped it was him. I couldn't see that it was. You start thinking stupid things in the dark. 'I can't see,' I said. 'I keep tripping over.'

'Give me your hand,' Mick said. We felt about in the dark until our hands collided, and our fingers wrapped warmly together.

I asked, 'Shall we sing, "He who would valiant be?"'

Mick laughed, and started singing it, so I joined in. Neither of us is a very good singer. We felt our way down the passage to the bottom of the stairs, with me keeping close to Mick and trying to tread where he trod, because he knew all the warped boards. At the bottom of the stairs we stopped and looked up, and we could see the moonlight shining through the landing window, turning the wall white and edging the banister and steps in white too.

' "Hobgoblin nor foul fiend shall daunt our spirits!" ' I said.

Mick turned to me, and the moonlight was so bright that, even though we were at the bottom of the stairs, I could see his face faintly. 'They'll be there tonight,' he said. And he started to climb the stairs, pulling me after him by the hand.

I went up the stairs after him, but the closer we got to the landing and its window, the less I wanted to look out into the moonlight and the dark. I said, 'Come on Mick. Don't let's be silly. Let's go back to the kitchen.'

'Just have a look through the window,' Mick said. 'Then you'll see.'

'I don't want to look through the window,' I said. I think, if I lived at Dancers, I'd only ever look out of the windows on the other side of the house, the ones that look over the valley, the factories and the power-station.

The stairs at Dancers are steep, but there aren't many of them. Mick was almost at the landing window. I pulled at his hand. 'No, come on Mick. I believe you,' I said. 'I don't need to look.'

'Look anyway,' he said. 'I thought you wanted to know why Dancers is called Dancers?' He stepped on to the landing.

I let go of his hand and stood on the stairs below him.

He put both hands on the sill and looked through the window. He looked, and sighed, and then smiled at me. 'Ar, there they be,' he said. 'They'm always there.' He looked through the window again. 'There's Lou . . . Come up and see Lou,' he said to me.

I backed down a step. 'I'd rather . . . rather not, Mick.'

'There's nothing to be scared of. Come and look, and then tell me I was dreaming.'

I went down another step. 'I'd better be getting home, Mick. Got to be up early tomorrow.'

'Come here and see the dancers!' he said.

I went all the way back down the stairs. 'Sorry Mick. Got to go. I'll be seeing you – goodbye!'

And I blundered down the dark passage, bumping into the walls, and I got out of Dancers and on to the road. I was glad that the hedges were so high that I couldn't see the little hill Mick's dancers danced on.

I climbed the road to the top of the hill, and walked through the estate of new houses. I was glad to see the moonlight shining on the chrome of the cars, and the electric lights shining red and blue through the drawn curtains. I stopped among the pretty gardens at a place where I could look over the valley with all its electric lights. I could see, on the hills across the valley, the red lights marking the television masts; and an aeroplane winked red and green lights at all the lights below it. I like to see those lights: they're bright, they're beautiful, and not even the cleverest people alive can tell you what electricity really is.

I didn't think that I'd be going back to Dancers for a long time. I didn't want to be persuaded to look through the window. I couldn't stand it if I looked, and saw nothing on Dancer's hill but hawthorns.

The Dreamer

Occasionally, after the local press has printed an article about me and, as they irritatingly do, published my full address, I've had oddballs turn up on my doorstep. They want me to put aside my work and write at length about them, or their favourite hobby-horse. When I opened the door to find a young woman standing on my doorstep clutching a clipping about me, I assumed she was another one.

She asked me if she could come in, and I couldn't think of a polite way to refuse her. She walked down my hallway, hugging herself, and sat primly on the edge of a chair when I invited her to sit. She wasn't someone you would have noticed if she hadn't invited herself into your house. Her face was pleasant, but plain; her hair was brown and hung limply to her shoulders, with no style. Her clothes, too, were limp and drab: a navy-blue skirt that might have been part of an old school uniform, and a thin, pale-blue jumper with long sleeves and a round neck – the most boring kind of jumper you can find. And though she was quite young – probably no older than twenty – there was something slow and tired about her movements and manner, as if she was much older than she looked.

I asked her if she wanted a drink, and she said that a cup of tea would be lovely. I went into the kitchen to make it, leaving her alone, sitting on the very edge of her chair, her knees pressed together, and her body bent over her hands clasped in her lap, and the clipping spread on the table before her.

When I returned, and asked what I could do for her, she seemed to find it difficult to begin talking, which surprised me. Most oddballs are so full of themselves and their obsessions that chat flows out of them. It's hard to follow, because they make no allowance for the fact that you don't know what they're talking about, but at least they don't sit staring at their cup in your living room, interrupting your day with silence.

I gave her no encouragement, maliciously thinking that if she'd taken it upon herself to come, she could also take on responsibility for the conversation. I sipped at my own tea, and watched her, and waited. She glanced up at me now and again, and smiled in embarrassment.

'I read your book,' she said. 'I liked it.'

'Thank you,' I said, without bothering to ask which of my books she was talking about.

'I thought . . . I thought, it being that kind of book . . .' She looked up bravely, almost glaring at me. 'I thought, if you'd written that, you'd understand.'

I smiled slightly. I had no idea what she was talking about.

'Can I tell you what happened to me?' she asked.

'Please.'

'There was this dream I had,' she said. 'I live in Lutley Street – you know it? It's just down the road, a couple of streets away. It's a council house we live in. It's a bit crowded – there's me, me Mum and Dad and three brothers. And a cat. I got a job in a supermarket when I left school, just on the tills, but then they put me in for their management scheme. I really wanted to do well on that 'cos I'd never been much at school. I was ever so surprised when they asked me to go on it.'

'This was a dream?' I asked, a bit confused. She ignored me.

'We've got this tree in our garden,' she said. 'A big old apple tree. It has beautiful blossom on it. Anyway, it was this really lovely spring weather. Only May, but the sun was shining, it was really warm. It was my day off and I thought, I won't waste this lovely sunshine, I'll go and sit out in the garden. We had this sun-lounger. I set it up under the apple tree and I sat out there with my magazine and a cup of coffee. It was really relaxing and lovely. And I fell asleep, the way you do in the sun. It must only have been a few minutes . . . But I get so mixed-up about this.'

I leant my head in my hand.

'Anyway, when I woke up . . . I knew I'd been dreaming . . . Nothing was like it had been. Well, there was an apple tree – but there was no garden, and no house. No street. There *was* a house, I should have said, but not *my* house . . . It was bigger and older and it was by itself . . . There was no street. There was a yard, and sheds . . . And things piled about. And past the yard, there were fields. It was a farm.

'I got up – I'd been sitting in a chair – and I wandered round this yard. And I started to think: you're dreaming. But I'd never had a dream before where I'd known I was dreaming . . . I didn't know what to think. I felt all peculiar. I went around this yard, and I looked into sheds and barns, and I could feel everything – oh, rust on an old rake, and hard wooden handles, and I got stung by a nettle, and it all felt like it should, you know? And I could smell everything, and everything looked right, you know? Right colours, right shapes and sizes. It wasn't like a dream at all. It was real. So I went to the house, and went inside and it was like – it was like I knew the place and didn't know it at the same time, you know? I mean, I knew it, I knew everything about it, but I sort of didn't expect to see it – and it all seemed really clear, every little mark and stain and colour, like when you're a bit woozy from booze. I went into the kitchen, and there was Kathleen and Jen – I knew them, knew their names, but I was surprised when I saw them – and they said, "You've been asleep in the sun! Your nose is all red!" See, they knew me too.'

She stopped and looked at me hard, looking for the understanding she'd thought she'd find in me. I was wondering just how mad she was, and had nothing to say. After a moment she went on.

'I said, "I fell asleep – but I've shelled all the peas. I've left 'em outside though." "Oh, you – you'd forget your head if it was loose," Kath said. And I went outside and fetched the peas. And then I helped them make the dinner. I knew them. Jen was my sister, and Kathleen was my sister-in-law and, if anything, I liked Kathleen better than Jen. Anyway, the more I talked with them, the more I knew I'd just been dreaming. All that about the council house and training to be a manager – it sort of broke into little pieces and drifted away, the way a dream does. Sort of got lost, scrap by scrap . . . And I forgot about it. It was just one dream among all the hundreds you have. It wasn't even a bad dream – or a special one. Nothing about it, really, to remember.

'I lived on this farm with my mother and father and sister, and my brother and Kath lived with us and . . . Well, I don't want to bore you to death. I met a bloke at a dance and married him about eighteen months later. In television repair, he was, and we moved to the town. I liked it there. More going on than in the country, you know. And we had three kids, lovely kids. We was really lucky. Nothing seemed to go wrong for us, you know. You hear of some people, the bad luck they have, all their lives. So we felt really lucky.'

There was a change about her. She'd relaxed, sitting straighter instead of hunching over her knees, and her voice had become firmer.

'It wasn't all tea-dances. Me Dad died, and that did hit me hard. But me brother carried on with the farm, and me mother lived with them . . . Our kids used to go out and stay with 'em a lot, help 'em with the work. It was nice, that, the kids having the farm to go to. My eldest, that was what he wanted to do, estate management . . . Me daughter did well, married a doctor, and her was expecting—'

She broke off, abruptly bowed forward over her knees again and began to cry. I sat sharply forward myself and didn't know what to do. I was angry with her for coming to my house and sobbing. 'Are you all right?' I said. I might as well have kept silent. She wept on, and I crouched there, embarrassed, on the edge of my chair.

Eventually she looked up, and wiped at her eyes with her fingers. 'I'm sorry. I shouldn't make an exhibition of myself. But there's my daughter expecting, and my youngest still needing me – and I go and wake up. I woke up, and I was on the sun-lounger under the apple tree in Lutley Street. I only remembered that dream when I woke up in it! I keep waiting for it to go away, but it's been nearly a year now . . . I used to take sleeping pills, hoping I'd dream and wake up – but I only have stupid dreams about wandering through corridors or being chased by tigers, and I wake up *here* every time and I don't want to be here . . . I even wrote to the farm, but it came back, "Address Unknown".'

'But,' I said, 'it was the farm that was the dream, surely?' It had to be, didn't it? Because if the farm was real and Lutley Street a dream, then the house we were sitting in, my books, my garden, were all simply part of her dream. And worse, my whole life, my school-years, my wearisome adolescence, my happier adult-hood, my little bit of success, my little bit of fame – they were all part of her dream too. And that couldn't be.

'That's what they tell me,' she said. 'My family, their doctor . . . But I had my whole life in what they call a dream. I grew up on that farm. I courted. I married and I loved my husband. And my lovely kids – and I can't see my daughter's little babby . . . What's happened to them?' She suddenly reached towards me, and I hastily drew back, as if her touch could annihilate me. 'Have I died?' she demanded. 'Is this death?'

Mad, I thought. How can I get rid of her?

'In your book, you said that what we see in dreams is real. You said dreaming was seeing other worlds. Do you really think that?'

I got up from my chair so that I could get further away from her. 'It was only a book,' I said. 'I just wrote what I thought would make the story work.'

'I want to be in the world where I was married and had my whole family,' she said. 'I don't want to be in this one. How do I get out of this one? How do I dream the right kind of dream?'

'Don't ask me,' I said. I was wondering how I could ask her to leave without annoying her. Who knew how she might react if I annoyed her?

She sat there in my chair, upright, quiet, her face pulled into an ugly, rigid expression, a grin of misery. Tears ran down her face.

'You could look at it this way,' I said, as gently as I could. 'In that dream your life was nearly over. In this one, you're still young. You've got a whole other life to live.'

She heard this in silence, then suddenly stood up. 'I'll go,' she said. 'I won't waste any more of your time.' Evidently, I had not understood as she had hoped I would.

I saw her to the front door, said goodbye politely. She didn't reply. I was glad to shut the door on her. I remember leaning on the door and thanking God I was rid of her.

But I'm not. I can't stop thinking about her. I can't stop savouring the conviction with which she told her story. She knew it to be true. And she didn't ramble; she didn't speak half-sense or make any of the strange remarks of the mad, which seem as if they ought to mean something, but mean nothing.

She knew her story was true. I keep thinking of her young face and her listless, old movements, her slow, old voice. I find myself believing her. I immediately shake myself mentally, and tell myself it's impossible – well, of course it's impossible. But the flavour of truth remains. Something in me knows it's the truth.

When you sit in a room, you can see three walls. How do you know that the wall you can't see, the one behind you, is still there? You suppose it is, you remember that it is, you believe that it is. But how do you *know* that it is? Of course, when you turn round, the wall is always there. But was it, a second before you turned round? And the wall that is behind you now that you've turned round – is *that* still there?

And I once had to get up early to catch a train. The alarm clock rang, I got up, washed, dressed, ate breakfast, set out for the bus-stop – and then woke up. I'd only dreamed that I'd dutifully got myself up. So, in a panic, seeing I was late, I jumped out of bed, washed, dressed, ate a quick breakfast, dashed out of the house – and woke up. I had plenty of time. I had only dreamed that I was late. I took my time about getting up, washed, dressed, ate, strolled out of the house – and woke up. I don't know how many times I dreamed that rising: each time it was real in every particular. Only a strange pungency, an abrasive smell of hot bedroom, a jarring strike on the ear of the alarm clock's electronic squall told me that I had, at last, woken in reality – or so I believed.

I used that dream within dream experience when I wrote my fantasy of walking in other worlds. A dream, I told myself, *is* another world, completely real. It helped to write the book, but I didn't believe it.

I should, as the woman said, have understood.

But if she was telling the truth, then I, and all the world that I suppose to be real and solid, am no more than a small, unimportant part of the dream that she's dreaming, not even part of the main action. What happens to me when she wakes up?

Or perhaps we are both, she and I, part of the dream of another dreamer. At any moment in our lives, even the best moment, that dreamer might wake and—?

It's stupid to be unsettled by such an incredible story. I should be able to say: she was mad, poor woman, and dismiss her entirely. But I keep remembering dreams that I've had . . . the dream where I was trapped in the cave, with the sea coming in fast through the cave entrance. The utter reality of it; the cold, the weight of drenched clothes, the slap of water, the completeness of the sounds and their quality. The knowledge that I was going to drown and the desperate fear. Utterly real. If I sleep, or if she wakes, will I be in that world again? Will I drown there?

I fear to sleep. I fear to wake. I expect, every moment, to see the world vanish and – what? What do the inhabitants of a dream see when their dreamer wakes?

Hiders Can Find

I always loved teasing her.

Before we were married, I gave her a birthday present. I got one of those large boxes that baked beans come in by the gross, and I covered the ugly lettering with gold paper, and wrapped it in more pretty paper, with ribbon bows.

She must have spent twenty minutes admiring the box, looking at me with big eyes, and saying it was a pity to spoil it by opening it. I enjoyed every moment, every look, every sigh, every inane repetition – not only because she was pretty and I loved her, but because I knew what was coming.

After I'd encouraged her by untying one of the ribbons, she opened the box. Inside was a lot of tissue paper which she threw on the floor, and a smaller parcel wrapped in blue metallic paper.

She took this parcel on her lap and gave me another wide-eyed, blushing look. Ha, ha, I thought: wait till you open it. Inside the blue parcel was more wadding and another parcel, wrapped in silver paper. Inside that was another parcel, wrapped in shiny red paper, and inside that, another gold parcel.

You get the idea. After two more parcels had been unwrapped she began to say things like, 'It must be fragile to need so much wrapping!' and, 'Good things come in small parcels!'

The parcels became very small. When she finally reached the last one, it held a gob-stopper.

Her disappointment was tasty, and even more so her attempt to disguise it. Of course, she'd been expecting something small and valuable – like a ring.

Well, I thought, that'll teach you to count your chickens.

She remembered her manners the instant the disappointment flickered across her face, and she smiled, bobbed her head and crammed the gob-stopper into her mouth. 'Best birthday present I ever had! Just what I wanted!'

Then I took the flat, unwrapped box from my pocket. When she opened that, there was a necklace inside, a rather expensive one, to make up for the gob-stopper. I was acclaimed as sweet and a rotten tease. 'You wait until your birthday!'

After our marriage I went on teasing: by then it was expected of me. Pretending I'd forgotten our anniversary, then springing the surprise. Pretending I was just going to give her a record token for Christmas because

I was too busy to go shopping, and then producing the expensive perfume. But it became too predictable: the disappointments no longer disappointed her; the surprises no longer really surprised.

So I started a new game. She knew nothing about it, so her response was always fresh and enjoyable. And I didn't have to wait for birthdays and holidays.

I came in from work one day and saw her purse lying on the phone table in the hall. I put the purse in my pocket and, since I was going straight up to the bathroom, I carried it upstairs with me and hid it at the back of the airing cupboard.

All that evening I waited, with excited patience, for her to notice that her purse was missing. Agonising. I was on edge, my skin felt prickly. My heart kept jumping into fast spurts. I hadn't had such a kick from being around her for ages. Every time she spoke, I jumped, thinking she was going to say something about her purse. But it wasn't until about nine o'clock, when she was putting her things ready for work the next morning, that she started fussing from room to room, looking under cushions, behind chairs, among cups on the kitchen dresser.

'What are you looking for?' I asked, grinning all over my face – she wasn't looking at me.

'My purse. Have you seen it?'

At last, I thought. At last she was doing just what I'd

guessed she would. It made me feel good. I got up and started to help her look for it. We searched the lower floor exhaustively. Her handbag was turned out and all her pockets. Cupboards, shelves, sills and drawers were cleared. We found a lot of change, combs, old envelopes and hair-grips, but no purse.

'Where did you last have it?' I asked, glowing inside.

'I had it in my hand when I came in because I'd just taken my keys out of it . . . I usually put it on the table.'

'It must still be on the table then.'

'No, I've looked . . . Anyway, I think I put it down by the phone.'

'Well, did you or didn't you? You must know!'

'I thought I did . . . but it's not there, so—'

We didn't give up the search until nearly twelve, when I made some coffee. She was almost in tears by then. All her money and her credit cards, her season ticket – all the things she needed for the next day – were in the purse.

'I shall have to phone in a minute and cancel my cards,' she said. 'It's a twenty-four hour service, isn't it?'

When I thought of all the hassle of getting the cards replaced, I almost broke. I could have started another search and triumphantly found the purse. But, as my mother used to say, 'Hiders can always find.' I'd give myself away. And it would certainly be more fun to let things go on.

'You must have lost it,' I said. 'Put it down somewhere and forgot to pick it up. Trust you. I can lend you some money for tomorrow.'

'Thanks. But I could swear I had that purse with me when I came home.'

She kept saying that. The next night she gave me a minute by minute account of the purse's whereabouts during the previous day, ending with it being in her hand when she closed the front door behind her.

'It must be in the house! If I'd lost it, I wouldn't have had the keys to open the door!'

'That's true,' I agreed, and we started another detailed search of the house. This time she even searched upstairs as thoroughly as down – except that she didn't think to look behind the sheets at the back of the airing cupboard.

I was surprised that it was all going so well. I half expected her to guess that I'd hidden it, and to accuse me, and as the evening dragged on I began to feel disappointed in her. But I suppose I'd never played a trick on her quite like this.

'I had it in my hand when I came through the door, I know I did. I'd just taken my keys out of it.'

If she'd really lost her purse, her constant repetition of these facts would have irritated me. As it was each time she said, yet again, that she was sure she'd put it down by the phone, was a moment of pure joy to me.

It must have been more than a month later, after all her plastic had been replaced, that she came down from the bathroom with a towel wrapped round her head, the purse in her hand, and a stunned expression on her face.

'My purse,' she said.

'Well?'

'No – my old one. The one I lost.'

I converted the joy I felt into an appearance of amazement. 'Where did you find it?'

'In the airing cupboard. Right at the back. Everything's here – money, cards, keys . . . I didn't put it in the airing cupboard. I couldn't have.'

'Well, I didn't,' I said, feeling an inward quiver that was part fear of being caught out, and part pleasure.

'How did it get there?'

'Maybe it walked up the stairs and climbed in by itself.'

'Oh, come on – hey.' She gave me a long look.

'What?'

'It wasn't you, was it?'

'What?'

'Hid it – as a joke?'

My heart began to beat faster. I felt my face begin to redden, and I tried to look and sound annoyed. 'Some joke! Look, I might have hid it, if I'd thought of it. But I'd have damn well told you where it was before you'd had new keys cut and new credit cards and all that trouble.'

'Yes, you would,' she said. 'Sorry.' She was as easy as that to fool. I loved the apology.

'But how did it get there?' She stood looking at the purse in her hand. 'I suppose I must have put it there. I must have been looking for a towel or something. I can't remember . . . I must have had a brainstorm.'

Lovely!

And there were infinite possibilities for this game. Her job – she sold computers – meant that she spent nights away almost every week. So I had the house to myself, and I could move, or hide, or alter what I liked.

I'd move her perfume from her dressing table to the bathroom cupboard, and then, when she was looking for it, swear I knew nothing about it.

'Oh, is this it?' I'd call from the bathroom. 'I thought I'd noticed it in here.'

She'd come trailing in. 'But I never put it in there . . .'

I'd move the house plants to different places, and then say, 'I haven't touched them. You know I can't tell one from another.'

'But I know I haven't moved it . . .'

Sometimes I'd draw her attention to a change. 'Why

have you moved all the dishes round in the kitchen? I can't find anything.'

I said I'd pay the telephone bill and didn't, and then, when the reminder came, I'd swear blue oaths that she'd said she'd pay it.

'I was going to,' she said, 'but you said you'd do it, remember?'

'That was the time before last, love. This time, you were going to pay it. We decided that.'

Trying hard to control her exasperation and angry tears, she said, 'As far as I remember, we decided that you were going to pay it.'

'As far as you remember,' I said. 'That's no doubt why it hasn't been paid. Look, let's not argue about it. I'll write the cheque and we'll forget it.'

'That seems to be what I'm good at – forgetting. I'm not thirty yet. What is this? Galloping senility?'

'Don't worry about it,' I said, so generously that she apologised to me again. It was cream.

Some tricks I came up with off the cuff. There was the time she asked me to copy down a telephone number for her. I altered one of the digits, and then insisted I'd copied it down exactly as she'd called it out. After a bit of argument, I conceded that I might have made a mistake, but by then she was already half convinced that she'd been the one who'd made the mistake, and said, no, no, I was probably right; she just hadn't been concentrating. She was becoming very wary of trusting her own memory or judgement. 'What do you think?' she'd ask earnestly, and, 'Remind me.' This was something I hadn't foreseen, this loss of confidence, but – it was interesting. I couldn't help but wonder how far I could push it.

After a year of my special treatment, she turned down a promotion at work. They asked her to become manager of her Mickey-Mouse department, and she said no. 'I couldn't handle it. I was surprised they asked me.'

'Why shouldn't they ask you?' I said, ever the loyal, supportive hubby.

'Well, you know – I'm so forgetful.'

I kissed her cheek. 'It's a good job I like you absent-minded.'

But they talked her into taking the management job in the end. They made her feel that she had a responsibility to the firm, and then they sent her on presentation courses – how to sell yourself as well as the product, that sort of baloney. I know she was in a panic about it, but she was excited as well, because all the persuasion and pressure at work had made her feel important.

'I don't want you selling yourself,' I said.

She waggled her hips and rolled her eyes. 'I'd get a good price though, eh?'

Her boss was sending her memos, telling her how good she was at her job, and she got like this – high and grinning all the time, and full of answers.

I stole her car keys and dropped them down a drain to get rid of them for good. She didn't make as big a fuss as usual. She took a taxi, charged it to the firm, and bought another set of keys.

I hid cups and plates. I put a joint of meat back in the freezer after she'd taken it out to thaw. I cancelled a timer programme she'd made on the video. I threw her clothes all over the bedroom. I emptied a plant-pot on the carpet. And she said, 'You know, we've got a poltergeist.'

This took *me* by surprise, I must admit. 'A what?'

'Look at this mess. You didn't do it, I didn't do it . . . And all the things that keep being moved and then put back, or that just disappear forever . . . I know you're going to say it's silly, but we've got a poltergeist.'

I started wondering whether this notion would improve my game or spoil it.

'I was talking to a woman whose mother's house is haunted by a poltergeist. Seriously. She'd seen saucepans flying through the air. She said her mother was used to it, took it for granted.'

'I've yet to see any flying saucepans.'

'Maybe that's for the future.'

I was never certain whether she actually believed we were haunted, or whether she was using the idea of a poltergeist to hide the fact that she'd found me out, but either way my game was spoiled. She always referred to the poltergeist as Fred. What else? She was never original.

When she came down in the morning to find the front and back doors standing open she called out, 'Oh Fred! Shut doors after you!' When pages were removed from her personal organiser, she said, 'Fred, if you don't leave my things alone, I shall have you exorcised!'

I suppose I should have stopped playing until she'd forgotten the poltergeist excuse, but I was too much in the habit. And it annoyed me to see every trick I thought of dismissed with some squeal about Fred. She actually liked the idea of having a poltergeist around the house. It made her feel special, I think. Psychic, or something.

My shaving brush disappeared. I stood in the bathroom, staring blankly at the spot where it should have been, where it always was, and slowly realising that I had half an hour to get ready for work, and the whole house to search. A quick search of the bathroom – including the airing cupboard – told me that it probably wasn't in the bathroom. Might be, but probably wasn't.

I thought of every place it might be: all those scores of hiding places I'd found for her things. Any pocket of any coat or jacket in the house. Any shoe. The pantry, among all those packets and jars. Any shelf. Under or behind any chair. Balanced on top of a curtain rail. In any drawer.

I was furious. I stood there thinking: how dare she? How dare she?

I opened the bathroom door and called, 'Seen my shaving brush?'

'I don't shave,' she called back. Just the kind of answer I might have given.

'It's gone. I can't find it.'

'Oh Fred, you naughty poltergeist, playing with master's things!' she said.

A veiled accusation. I forced a laugh and went without a shave.

That evening, my shaving brush was back in its usual place. 'You found my shaving brush, then?' I said.

'Is it back? I didn't. Fred must have returned it.'

I didn't admit anything. I went on playing my game and she went on playing hers. After my first anger died down, it was interesting. Less fun than when I'd played on my own, but interesting.

She was away, staying overnight in Liverpool, when I returned home to find written, in lipstick, on the bathroom mirror, 'I can see you.'

A good one, I thought, reading it. A hint of a threat, but it could also be read as a flat statement, a warning or a taunt . . . but when had she written it? She'd left for Liverpool straight from work the afternoon before – she'd said. So the words must have been on the mirror the night before when I'd stood in front of them to brush my teeth, and that morning when I'd shaved. Impossible. I couldn't have missed them.

I admit to a few moments of unease, the kind you get when you think there's a stranger in your house. Then I started to rationalise. I must just have missed the lettering. Perhaps the light had fallen differently, and I might have been tired . . . She'd often missed things I'd hidden in plain view.

Another explanation, of course, was that she wasn't in Liverpool. She'd either never gone, or she'd come home early, to write this message for me.

Except that she phoned me that evening, from Liverpool, to tell me that she was too tired to drive home, and she'd see me the next day, after work. At least, she said she was phoning from Liverpool.

So I spent another night alone and returned home the next evening to find the hall filled with steam. In the kitchen a kettle was boiling on a lit gas-ring, and the teapot stood ready on the dresser, filled to the top with tea-bags. I switched the kettle off and opened the door and windows before looking over the rest of the house.

She wasn't there, but the gas fires were turned on, and the chair I usually sat in was pushed right against the television. Upstairs in the bathroom not only my shaving brush was missing, but also my soap, my razor, my aftershave and my toothbrush.

Obviously she was taking revenge for all my tricks at once. I'd never been so unsubtle.

When she let herself in later that night I was in control of my temper. 'How was Liverpool?' I asked her, and got a long account of the terrible journey, the really nice hotel, the nasty customers and how tired she was and how there was no place like home.

A truthful account? Or calculated to seem truthful?

'My shaving brush has gone missing again,' I said. 'And a lot of other things. You don't know anything about it, do you?'

'It's *Fred*,' she said. 'I've read up about poltergeists. They usually stop of their own accord after a while.'

Her tone convinced me that she was responsible for it all. So she hadn't been in Liverpool. She'd been hiding somewhere nearby. At a hotel or with a friend: maybe with a man. But it wasn't so much the thought of her being with another man that infuriated me as the thought that she'd lied to me, sneaked in while I was asleep, played tricks on me – tricks that had worked and had even thrown a scare into me. The trickster tricked! Corny, I know. I should have been bigger about it, I know. But it was so galling.

'OK,' I said, sitting on the arm of a chair. 'Shall we cut

the poltergeist crap? You weren't in Liverpool. Where were you?'

She gave a good imitation of astonishment. 'Where was I?'

I told her about the writing on the mirror, the kettle, the teapot and the chair.

'I was in Liverpool,' she said. 'You can check up with the firm if you don't believe me . . . Maybe we should bring someone in. Ghost researchers, you know.'

'I don't believe in ghosts.'

'How can you not?' she said, and smiled.

I was on the edge of saying, look, I played these tricks before you. But though I took a breath ready to say it, I couldn't say it. I would be giving away too much.

'I find it hard to believe,' I said lamely.

'But they're quite common,' she said, looking me in the eye. 'I read about them in a magazine.'

Bitch, I thought. I never would have thought she could be a better player than me. She had me tied in a knot. I couldn't do anything to stop her making a fool of me without revealing what I had done – and so making a fool of myself.

I began to be very careful of my things. I'd hide them myself – and sometimes forget where. Or they were taken from the places I'd hidden them and hidden again somewhere else. And there were always the things

I couldn't hide. Coins went missing from the pockets of the clothes I was wearing – or I thought they did. Perhaps I was becoming paranoid? The new razor I'd bought and secretly hidden in a case on top of my wardrobe was missing the very next morning, even though I was certain she couldn't have known it was there. A lucky find on her part?

She was spending the night in London when I was woken by the smell of smoke. I got up and went round the house. As soon as I opened the living-room door, I felt the heat, and the smoke was choking. The curtains were on fire. The flames were climbing up them towards the ceiling. I stood there, staring. Then I almost fell, in running for the kitchen and a bowl of water.

I don't know how many times I ran backwards and forwards in a sweat of panic. I managed to put the fire out – and drenched myself and the room – but God, it shook me up. And almost the worst of it was wondering: does she want to burn me alive? Have I gone too far: does she hate me?

That was terrifying. I'd never meant her any harm. I'd teased her, yes. I'd enjoyed watching her flap and fuss over things I'd moved or hidden. But I'd never done or meant her any harm.

I would have preferred not to say anything about the fire to her – after all, she knew about it – but the scorch marks and the burned curtains made that impossible. 'My God,' she said, clutching at her face, 'what happened?'

'Your poltergeist is getting out of hand.'

'Fred did this? We should move into a hotel.'

'Let's just sleep lightly,' I said. I felt fairly safe while she was in the house with me.

She went up to bed early, and I sat up, wondering what I could do to get even. I could creep up and set fire to her bed – except that I never wanted to hurt her, as it seemed she wanted to hurt me.

A thump made me look round. A book had fallen off the bookcase and was lying open on the floor. There was no reason why it should have fallen and, just for a moment, I felt afraid – but then I went over and picked the book up, closed it and laid it down flat on a shelf.

As I turned away, I heard it fall again.

Then I was scared. The book couldn't have fallen. She was upstairs. How was she doing it? By wires?

I turned and looked at the book. It was lying open. It was an old book, the layout old-fashioned. I read the title at the top of the page. *Our Time in Tibet.* I couldn't remember ever having seen it before. I hadn't bought it, and it didn't seem the kind of book that she would choose to read.

I closed it, put it back on the shelf and stood watching it.

The book lay there, oblong and solid and quite still,

and I stood staring myself cross-eyed at it until I felt like a fool. I also began to feel comforted. It was just a book. Someone might have given it to one of us, and we'd forgotten it. And so it had fallen – so what? Things fall. I turned away and immediately the book fell again.

I looked back and there it was, lying open on the floor. I felt my scalp chill and the cold ran on down my back. I knew the book was going to be open at the same page, and I was afraid to check in case it was. I wanted to go away, to go upstairs – but to leave the book lying there would be unbearable.

I slowly went into a crouch and picked the book up. It felt very slightly warm to the touch, and it was open at the same page.

'In Tibet we were told the quaint tale of the bowler hat,' I read. 'It seems an erstwhile Western visitor came with a bowler hat. As he was traversing one of the windy mountain passes, the wind lifted the bowler from his head and deposited it much further down the steep mountain in a place too inaccessible for recovery. And there the bowler hat remained.

'The Tibetans, passing on the mountain paths, could see the bowler in the undergrowth but couldn't imagine what it was, never having seen its like before. Its sinister, crouching aspect was such that they quickly concluded it to be an evil spirit or minor demon. They took to hurrying past the spot, heads bowed over folded hands, muttering prayers to protect them against the bowler's malevolence. And this belief – for fear argues strong belief – had a startling effect on the lost bowler – the hat became endowed with vitality! The bowler took to prowling along the mountain paths, drinking at streams and stealing food from villages. To this day, say the locals, it can be seen quietly pursuing its mysterious purposes among the mountain meadows. This shows, they say, how powerful is belief.'

I straightened my now aching legs. Carefully I closed the book and put it back on the bookcase.

Written on the mirror: 'I can see you.'

All through the house, on the floor above my head, in every corner, swelling in the room around me, I could feel silent laughter.

My chair pushed against the television set; the teapot full of tea.

The curtains on fire.

Her belief had created it, not mine. And it didn't like me.

Emily's Ghost

In a part of the lane that was screened from the houses by tall trees and hedges, Emily stopped and looked carefully around her. No one was in sight. A window was visible above the waving leaves of a tall elm, but there didn't appear to be anyone looking out. Satisfied that no one could see her, she began a frenzy of wriggling, wrenching at her clothes and hat.

The bones in her corset were digging into the flesh covering her ribs. The waistband of her skirt was tight. The many little buttons fastening her boots pinched, and their seams rubbed. Her hair was pulled back so tightly that the skin of her brow felt stretched, and the pain was considerable. One of the pins fastening her hat was scratching her scalp. And she was hot, bundled up in all those clothes, miserably damp and chafed and hot.

The thick material of her skirt and jacket resisted her fingers, and none of her fidgeting and pulling gave her any ease. Resigning herself to discomfort, she smoothed her skirt, tugged down her jacket, felt that her hat was at the correct angle, and all the time looked about for anyone who might have seen her. To her relief, there was still no one in sight. If her mother came to hear about her adjusting her clothes in the street, she would be lectured on Behaviour Proper in a Young Lady and The Importance of Not Letting Oneself Down.

She looked down the lane at the distance she still had to walk in the painful boots, and felt like crying. 'I think it would be a very good idea, Emily,' her mother had said, 'if you went by yourself to call on the Gordons. A ten minute call, to introduce yourself and welcome them to Oakham. Don't stay any longer. It would be good for you – you know, you will only lose this shyness if you *make* yourself meet people and talk with them. You may invite them to come to tea on – on – let's say Wednesday.'

'I shan't know what to say!' Emily had cried in alarm.

'What do you have to say? Only your name, and where we live, and that you hope they're settling in, and if there's anything we can do – that sort of thing. Then give Mrs Gordon one of our cards, and say that you must go, that you have other calls to make.'

'But I don't!' Emily had been taught that lying was a serious sin, but now, it seemed, she was required to lie.

'Well, what does that matter? It's politeness. You say you have other calls to make, and then you leave. Simplicity itself.'

'Oh, can't you go, mother?'

'No.'

'Why does anyone have to go?' Emily had demanded.

'Because someone *must*. How would you feel if you had just moved somewhere, and no one came to call on you? It's only polite. And besides, Mrs Gordon may have youngsters who will be nice friends for you. No, Emily,' she said, as Emily wailed in horror at this prospect of being shoe-horned into friendships. 'Don't argue; you shall go. It will be good for you.'

'What if Mrs Gordon offers me tea?' Emily grew quite wild-eyed at the thought of the teacups and the little plates of cake, and the prolonged conversation.

'She won't. She will know that you've only called to present your card. But if she does, you only have to do what I told you – say you have other calls to make, and must go.'

'She might think me rude!'

'Oh nonsense, Emily! Of course she won't! Now don't make this fuss, please! You know perfectly well how to behave – or have I been wasting my time all these years?'

'Can't you come with me?'

'No, I've decided. It's high time you started making calls by yourself, or what will you do when you have your own establishment?'

I won't call on anyone, that's what, Emily thought to herself in the lane. And I won't be at home to anyone. I won't leave these paper-chases of cards round the neighbourhood. I shall be renowned far and wide as a hermit.

A few more yards brought her to the gate of the villa where the Gordon family had newly taken up residence. She stopped, feet neatly together, and fiddled with the perfectly useless little bag she carried, which held nothing but a collection of visiting cards held together in a silver clip.

The corset-bones were still scratching her; the hatpin was still digging into her scalp. Her feet felt hot and swollen inside her boots, and indeed, she felt damp, warm and grubby all over. Most unsuitable company for polite society. How could she pay a visit in this state?

She contemplated walking a little further, to the milestone, and sitting on it for a while before simply going home . . . But her mother would discover that she hadn't made the call, and would be angry. There was no choice. She had to go through with it.

Lifting her head and setting her shoulders, she marched briskly between the brick gateposts and started up the drive. But before the drive's first bend, her walk had slowed, and when she came in sight of the big house, she stopped altogether. It was rather larger and grander than her house. The door would be answered by a maid, who would notice her damp, flushed face, and would leave her waiting in the hall while she fetched her mistress. And Mrs Gordon would no doubt be astonished to find a mere girl calling on her, and—

Emily felt so weighed down with the awfulness of her task that she wanted to sit down in the gravel. Why was life so full of nasty little errands like this one? Why did you always have to put on such uncomfortable clothes on such a hot day, and spend your time doing things you didn't want to do, while everything you did want to do was said to be unsuitable?

But it was impossible to go home. And it was impossible to stand there until she was seen from the window and the Gordons asked themselves what on earth that strange girl was doing in the drive. So, step by heavy step, she forced herself on to the porch, with its imposing door, and its stained glass. Raising an arm that felt made of stone, she rang the bell. And waited, feeling quite ill. And hot almost to fainting.

The wait was very long. Was it long enough for her to justify going home? 'No one came to the door, Mummy.' But just as she was gathering herself to go, the door was opened, by – as she had feared – a maid in black and white. She peered at Emily in what Emily felt to be a rebuking manner.

'I – I – I – I'm here to pay a call!'

'Come in, Miss.' Emily stepped into a dim and polished hall, her heart sinking into her nether regions as slowly and heavily as a large stone might sink into the mud at the bottom of a dark pond. Her heels clattered on a floor of black and white tiles. 'If you'd like to wait in here, Miss?' The maid held open the door of a nearby room.

'Oh – ah – thank you!'

'I'll just fetch mistress, Miss.' And the maid closed the door, and clattered away down the passage.

Emily stood in a large room, brightly lit by a bay window. The furnishings were rather sparse, but that was doubtless because the Gordons weren't settled yet. Her mother shouldn't have made her come! People didn't want callers before they'd even moved themselves into their house. Not only did she have to make conversation, but it would be conversation with a resentful and unwelcoming hostess. She ached to be away from that house.

There was a chair, and her feet hurt, but she didn't feel able to sit. What if Mrs Gordon came and found her making free with the chairs, without having been invited to sit? Nor did she feel able to move about the room. So she stood still just inside the doorway, feeling herself grow even hotter and damper, and worrying about what she would say when Mrs Gordon did arrive. She passed the time by imagining Mrs Gordon being dragged away from the unpacking of boxes to see her. 'Dratted callers!' she would be saying to herself, as she made her way from the very top of the house. 'Why do people have to pester you so?'

What shall I say to her? Emily thought, and tried out various sentences in her head. 'Good morning, Mrs Gordon; my mother sent me to call—' No, that sounded rude, as if she hadn't wanted to come. She hadn't, not at all, but that couldn't be admitted.

'Good morning, Mrs Gordon, I've come to leave my card—' No, that sounded so cold. But that was the only reason she had come. Oh, wasn't it stupid!

The sound of a footstep in the hall made her jump and her heart skitter. She turned to face the door, all damp and grubby and with untidy hair, and hadn't a clue what she might say when the door opened.

But the door didn't open. The footsteps went past and climbed the stairs. Emily was left to wait, and fret, for another interval.

Her hot feet throbbed in her narrow, high-heeled boots. If it would be impolite to sit in the chair without being asked, would it be permissible to perch on the window-seat? She thought it might, and went over to it. The view from the window was of flower beds and lawn, and she looked at it and longed to be out there, the call over, duty done.

Another noise from the hall. She shot to her feet, little bag clutched in front of her, and stared at the door so hard her eyes ached. The silly, strained expression faded from her face as she realised that no one was coming in. She had to wait again.

I can't bear this, she thought, as she seated herself on the window-seat again. Each renewed wait was worse than the one before it. She noticed that the window was standing a little open.

No wonder my mother despairs of me, she thought, as she pushed the window wide and climbed out. Her long, thick skirts dragged and rode up as she slithered over the sill, and she pulled at them in a panic, fearful that Mrs Gordon would come and catch her. Her corset-bones stabbed her viciously, and she was anxious in case some gardener or son of the house should come and see her exposed legs. But when she was outside, on the lawn, with her skirts shaken down, she began to giggle. She hadn't been caught! She'd got away with it!

She ran around the corner of the house and, avoiding the drive, dived into the shrubbery and pushed her way through until she was close enough to the gate to escape unseen. The branches tugged at her hat, ripping hairs from her scalp, but she clutched at it and battled on and, when she reached the road, her laughter was wild. She staggered as she went up the road, reeling with laughter. Her mother would have been mortified by the sight of her carefully raised daughter stumbling and roaring like a drunken sailor.

I didn't even leave a card, she thought, and giggled again, and pulled off the wretched hat, and its wicked hat-pin. 'And I don't care!' she said aloud to empty lane.

'I called, but the Gordons weren't in,' she said to her mother. No doubt she would be found out, but not today, and there was always hope that, somehow, it would be forgotten and she would get away with it.

'Did you leave a card?' her mother asked.

Emily bit her lip. 'Ah – no. I forgot.'

'Oh, Emily. What am I going to do with you?'

Emily's mother made the call herself the next morning. She came home and said, 'Mrs Gordon is one of those strange people who believe in ghosts. Oh well, I've invited them to tea in any case.'

So Mrs Gordon and her daughter came to tea on Wednesday afternoon. Mrs Brooke and her daughter received them. Emily envied Charlotte Gordon, who seemed perfectly happy. Perhaps she didn't wear corsets and had boots that fitted. Mrs Brooke was sure to observe, afterwards, that Charlotte Gordon's manners were everything that a young girl's ought to be – with a meaning look at her own daughter.

'Oh, Mrs Brooke,' Charlotte said, 'I do hope you can tell us something about our ghost!' Turning to Emily, politely including her in the conversation, the girl said,

'I've always wanted to live in a haunted house, but I never thought that I should!'

'Your ghost must be quite a newcomer too,' Mrs Brooke said. 'I never before heard of it.'

'Our maid saw it!' Charlotte said.

'Oh – maids!' said Mrs Brooke.

'I'm afraid it's perfectly true,' said Mrs Gordon, rather heavily, as she set down her teacup and lifted a slice of fruit-cake on to her plate. 'The maid answered the door to a knock and admitted a girl. She showed her into the drawing room and came to find me—'

'But when Mama came, she'd vanished!'

Mrs Brooke glanced briefly at Emily. 'Rude of her, certainly.'

'She hadn't left the room,' Charlotte breathed, leaning forward over her teacup. 'If she'd come out into the hallway, the maids would have seen her. And there was no other way out. She simply vanished.'

'Of course, the children are excited,' Mrs Gordon said. 'Has the ghost some dreadful secret she is trying to impart to us? Or is there treasure in the house and she's trying to tell us where it might be found? I said I would try and find out if there was any story in the neighbourhood.'

'None,' Mrs Brooke said firmly, with another straight look at her daughter. 'I'm afraid I'm one of those unfashionable people who don't believe in ghosts.'

'Oh, but she *couldn't* have left the room without being seen!' Charlotte said again. 'Really, she could not! So she must have been a ghost, mustn't she?'

'It's certainly hard,' said Mrs Brooke, 'to imagine how a young *lady* could escape from a closed room.'

'Do *you* believe in ghosts?' Charlotte asked Emily.

Emily, looking into her mother's eyes, said, 'Oh – yes! Yes! Firmly!'

The Wiz

A week earlier Sheila would have been delighted to hear that Kelly Davis was dead.

The headmistress continued, to the assembled school, 'It's a very great shock, I know. Kelly died in her sleep last night: she was found this morning. Her father phoned me a short while ago and asked me to pass the news to you before you heard it in any other way. We will say a short prayer for Kelly—'

Behind Sheila, there was whispering already:

'She never died in her sleep. She hung herself.'

'Never!'

'She did. Somebody told our mother this morning.'

Sheila fainted.

She woke up in the school's medical room, which was white and green and uncomfortable. 'Are you feeling better?' a woman said to her, an only faintly familiar woman. She managed to nod a little. 'Well, you lie there for a while,' said the woman. 'I'll come back and check on you later.' And she went quietly out of the room.

Sheila lay on the hard couch and she thought: Kelly is dead. For a long time she lay and thought: Kelly is dead. She couldn't think anything else; was afraid to think anything else.

A week before she would have been delighted to hear that Kelly was dead.

Kelly had been a tall, attractive girl, who had always seemed to know how attractive she was. Even at eleven, she had come to school in make-up, and as she'd grown older, the make-up had become more elaborate. But Sheila wouldn't have cared how much make-up and jewellery she wore, or how many times she flouted the school's dress code, if it hadn't been for Kelly's attitude towards anyone less attractive or less fashionable than herself. She despised them, and made sure they knew it. On the first day Kelly had met Sheila, when they had come from different schools to attend the same comprehensive, and had been put into the same class, Kelly had looked at Sheila and despised her. Ever since she'd made Sheila's life a misery.

In the first year it hadn't been too bad: a few incidents of name-calling. Even so, it had hurt enough for Sheila to avoid the other girl whenever she could. A mistake. Kelly had seen that, when attacked, it was Sheila's instinct to run away and hide. With every year, Kelly's taunts had become more frequent, more hurtful; and when Sheila still persisted in trying to avoid her, she had added slaps and punches. By the fourth year, persecuting Sheila was almost Kelly's hobby. Certainly, it relieved the boredom of school. Kelly, with her friends, would come looking for Sheila. Finding her, they would comment on her appearance minutely, and often wittily, drawing laughter from the boys Kelly usually had tagging along. Walking behind Sheila, Kelly would skilfully trip her, and had once succeeded in making her fall down a flight of concrete steps, skinning both knees and laddering her tights – which had caused hilarity among Kelly's crowd.

They came looking for her in the break, and at lunch-time, and after school. They tugged her bag away from her and scattered, even destroyed or stole, the contents. They pulled her hair or entangled chewing gum in it. 'You ugly stupid boring cow,' Kelly said, putting her face so close to Sheila's that their noses almost touched. 'Is there anybody here fancies this ugly boring cow?' And the boys laughed uproariously and made vomiting noises.

To the teachers, Kelly was quite different: bright and chatty, and the staff thought her charming. So Sheila knew it wasn't any use complaining.

She hated Kelly. It was because of Kelly that she felt sick when she got up in the morning. It was the thought of Kelly that made her shake as she set off down the road to school. She was always alone. She had never been all that good at making friends, and once Kelly had started her persecution, such friends as she had melted away. Kelly made her into such a loser that no one wanted to be her friend. She was ashamed even to try to make friends. Everyone thought her such a wimp.

Home was a sanctuary, a week's half-term holiday something that made it possible to get through the term. And it was during the half-term holiday that her dad had said to her, 'Like to come tonight, She?'

The usual fears had risen in her – that she would be out of place and merely tolerated by the people around her. But then she'd felt, defiantly, that if her father wanted her to go, why shouldn't she? What did it matter what anyone else thought? And it would be pleasant to go out, as other people did, to behave as if she had friends, to do something other than watch television with her mother.

So she'd gone in the car with her father to the pub where he was playing, The Perrot Arms. They'd arrived while the pub was still dark and quiet, the car-park empty, and the landlord had let them in the back way. Sheila had felt privileged to be in the behind-the-bar area, and to be helping the band carry microphones and cables. Not everyone could mix on such equal terms with the entertainment.

The band was setting up on the little stage in the lounge-bar. With only the bar-lights turned on, glinting softly on the bottles and optics, and the shadows hiding the flock wallpaper and garish carpet, it seemed an attractive place. The members of the band were all as old as her father, or older, and she felt comfortable among them. They smiled as they passed her, going backwards and forwards from the yard with equipment, and joked with her, and she began to feel quite lively and at ease. She'd always liked older people better than those of her own age. They were usually kinder. And they didn't seem to mind if you were stupid, ugly and boring.

'Oh, Joe can't make it,' Angelo said.

'So who's drumming?'

Angelo sat for a moment on one of the red, padded chairs, and scrubbed at his thinning hair. 'I got the Wiz,' he admitted.

There was a general groan from all the members of the band. 'Oh, hell, you didn't, did you?'

'He was all I could get!' Angelo said.

'Oh, brilliant!'

'I'm telling you, Ange, I want extra if I've got to put up with him for a whole evening.'

'He's a good drummer.'

Edging closer to her father, Sheila asked, 'Who is he?'

'Oh . . .' Her father was trying the valves on his saxophone. 'A right merchant banker, that's all. Thinks he's Merlin or a witch-doctor or summat.'

Harry, the trumpeter, who was sitting on the edge of the stage, laughed. 'He comes from Wolverhampton! Colin Evans.' He looked up as Sheila's father laughed. 'S'right. That's his name. I used to go to school with him. He was a right prat then an' all.'

'Hey up,' Angelo said warningly. The Wiz had just come wandering in. He came to a halt near the stage and stood looking up at Joe's drum kit.

'All right?' Angelo asked. 'Suit you?'

The Wiz nodded slowly. He wasn't very tall, but he was very thin. His legs, in their black jeans, were like clothed sticks, and the padded, checked shirt he wore over a black T-shirt hung baggy and unfitted. He was bearded, and his hair was shaggy and long, receding slightly from his brow, but long behind, hanging over his shoulders to below his hips. It was black, curly, and glistened as if oiled.

'Just time to get the drinks in, lads!' Angelo called, and the Wiz turned towards the bar, and towards Sheila. She saw that the other side of his face was painted black, the eye outlined with a white star. As she stared, her gaze met his, and she looked away. When she glanced back, he was still staring. He smiled and started towards her, except her father stepped in his way. 'That's my daughter,' her father said. 'The bar's over there, mate.'

The Wiz turned away and went to the bar, but he was still staring at Sheila as he went. He smiled and nodded.

Sheila looked away again. She was surprised at her father's intervention, but relieved. The Wiz looked far too strange a person for her to be able to cope with.

The landlord switched on more lights, and the bar became more like its brash self. The doors were opened, and the audience began to come in from the wet and darkness outside, bringing noise with them. They crowded up to the bar, and scattered among the tables to find a seat. The band, carrying their drinks, picked their way through to the stage and Sheila found herself a seat on a bench by the wall, right underneath her father as he stood on the stage. Angelo, on the piano, started to play a boogie-woogie, to cut through the noise and get the punters' attention.

After that, for almost an hour, Sheila enjoyed herself. The pub was warm and loud, the music fast and thumping. Everyone around her was in good humour, and she was lost in the crowd. She was able to tap her feet and her fingers in time to the music, and even sing along, without feeling that anyone was watching her, with a view to jeering at her clothes, or her singing out of tune, or some other small sin. When she looked up at the band, it was often to find the Wiz staring at her. She didn't understand why he was staring, and it gave her the creeps – but she didn't have to worry about him, because she was with her dad.

'Get me another half, love,' Harry said, handing his glass down to her. She went off to the bar, feeling pleased and important to be running the band's errands.

Then she saw Kelly and her friends come into the bar. A pang of fear and disappointment went through her, so sharp it felt as if she had actually been stabbed.

Kelly and her friends looked beautiful. They were made-up, and groomed, dressed in their best and glinting with jewellery, looking like models searching for a fashion shoot. They stood in a group at the back of the room, laughing loudly and glancing round to see who had noticed them laughing.

Sheila lowered her head and tried to be invisible. Having fought her way back from the bar through the close-packed tables, she was in her corner by the stage. Probably they wouldn't notice her. While keeping her head lowered, she peered from under her brows and watched them, as anything threatening is watched. She saw them grimace and laugh at the band. Trad Jazz, Fats Waller, Jelly Roll – that wasn't their style. Good, she thought. They'll leave the quicker. But, glancing up again, she saw Kelly looking straight at her. Kelly had seen her. Kelly spoke to her friends, nodded at Sheila, and grinned.

They left their place at the back of the room and started to push among the tables and chairs, trying to get closer to her. Sheila couldn't prevent herself from looking about for a way out. She felt panicky and trapped. But while the other girls were still struggling in the crowd, Sheila's father handed down his pint mug, and Sheila went off to get it filled. Kelly saw that, and she and her friends didn't try to get any nearer to Sheila's corner. But they stayed. They watched her hand the beer up to her father, and they waved to her and smiled.

'Friends of yours?' Angelo asked. 'Get us half a lager, love.'

They'll get tired, Sheila thought, as she edged through to the bar. They'd rather be getting off with boys than tormenting me. But fifteen minutes later, they were still there, laughing among themselves, sneering at the band and waving at Sheila. And then Sheila couldn't wait any longer, but had to go to the Ladies.

All the time she squatted in the cubicle she was listening, trying to tell if Kelly was outside. She heard people come into the lavatory, slam cubicle doors, splash in wash-basins, but she couldn't tell if any of them were Kelly. When she came out, of course, Kelly was waiting, leaning against a basin and grinning. And her friends were there, leaning and grinning, just as they did in school. Always leaning and grinning.

'Faugh!' Kelly said, fanning the air with her hand. 'What stinks? Have you farted, Jen?'

'Not me! My farts smell of roses.'

They laughed, looking at Sheila, who tried to get past them to the door. They moved slightly, enough to block her way.

'It must be you who stinks,' Kelly said to Sheila.

Sheila knew that whatever answer she made would be the wrong one, and made a more vigorous attempt to shove past them. That gave Kelly the excuse to shove back, to shove her hard against the sinks.

'Don't go throwing your weight around me!' Kelly said indignantly. 'Who does her think her is?'

Jen smirked and said, 'Her thinks her's somebody 'cos her dad plays in that twopenny-halfpenny band.'

'Which is he? The fat one with the trumpet?'

'They'm all old men.'

'Am they your pin-ups, Shei-la?'

It was hard to say why such childish gibes were so hurtful. Their predictability and witlessness was irksome. And it was so stupid to be afraid of them. She only had to get on the other side of that door and she would be back in the pub, and they wouldn't dare to do anything. For the third time Sheila pushed into them, determined to get past.

They pulled her hair. They kicked her. One of them flung a fist into her face and hurt her so much she thought her nose was broken. They shrieked, their voices ringing from the tiled walls. But Sheila got to the door and she got it open. She stumbled out into the bar, her hand at her nose.

People stared at her as she made her way back to her seat by the band. It was a while before she realised that her nose was bleeding. When she was sitting, shaking, in her seat, a woman leaned over and gave her a handful of tissues from her handbag.

Her father climbed down from the stage. The rest of the band would improvise around his absence. While the band's loud music thrashed on, he shouted at her, 'What happened to you?'

'Nothing,' she shouted back.

'Your nose is bleeding all down your face! You fall over, or what?'

'Yeah, I fell over.'

'Clumsy so-and-so. You all right?'

She assured him that she was, and he climbed back on the stage. She would have been ashamed to tell him the truth. Kelly and Jen and the others were standing at the back of the room again, laughing at her, and waving, nudging each other and giggling. Sheila felt physically sick, with anger and despair.

They left, after a few more minutes, but they'd ensured that Sheila could no longer enjoy the rest of the evening. She was trembling and, however much she tried to forget them, to concentrate on the music, her thoughts kept being drawn back to the shrieks, the laughter, the blows. She *hated* them. She would happily have seen them all dead.

Half-way through the evening the band took a break. While the others were shouting their orders at the bar, the Wiz sat down beside Sheila. He stretched his arms along the back of the bench, and said, 'They hit you. Them little tarts.'

'What?' she said.

He leaned towards her. 'I can fix 'em for you.'

She didn't like being teased and besides, there was a musty smell that hung about him. It reminded her of the animal cages at the zoo. 'No thanks.'

'Serious offer,' he said. 'There's a price. But I can fix 'em – so they'll never bother you again.' She looked up surprised. 'I was watching 'em. They been giving you trouble.' She didn't say anything. He smiled. 'I can fix 'em.' And then her father came to the table, bringing her a packet of crisps.

'All right?' he said to the Wiz, with a tinge of aggression in his tone.

'Got a packet for me?' the Wiz asked.

The second half of the evening dragged. Sheila wanted to go home, but her father was expecting her to go home with him and wouldn't approve of her catching the bus by herself. Not that she wanted to – Kelly and her friends might be outside. She set her teeth and endured.

'Time, gentlemen, time!' The band had played their last number, people were drinking their last drinks. Soon, Sheila told herself, soon – but she'd forgotten about the ritual of 'afters'. The lights were turned out, the bar emptied, the landlord locked up, and Sheila thought the band were staying behind simply to pack up their gear. But the landlord went out to the back of the pub and readmitted a small group who had left by the front door and walked straight round to the back. Her father nudged her and nodded towards a tall man in a camel coat. 'CID,' he said, and laughed.

Sheila sat on the edge of the stage and watched the band and the landlord's friends gather along the bar under the dimmed lights, and settle in for a long session of talking, drinking and smoking. 'Just a couple,' her father said to her; but she knew how just a couple could stretch out.

The Wiz came over and sat beside her. She glanced over at the bar, but her father was talking. The Wiz made her nervous; he was so weird with his long oiled hair and his painted face. She tried not to look at him, and to behave as if he wasn't there, hoping that this would make him go away. It didn't. He sat quietly beside her. Then he said, 'I can fix 'em. I can get 'em off your back.'

His persistence galled her. Still not looking at him, she said, 'No you can't.'

'I can.'

She dared to look him in the face. 'How?'

He returned her look steadily, until she looked away, blushing. She hated to blush.

'I'd spell 'em,' he said. He leaned back and crossed his legs, gazed up at the ceiling as if considering. 'I'd make a sending against them.'

From the bar, voices muttered, occasionally breaking into a laugh. Outside, cars crooned by. She waited for him to go on, but he didn't. She felt foolish, unable even to keep up her end of a conversation. So she cleared her throat and said, 'What's a sending?' She felt quite brave then, having said that.

He looked at her. 'If I make the spell, you got to pay the price.'

His tone had become sly, as if he was trying to trap her into something. She rose, meaning to go over to her father, but once on her feet decided that she was being cowardly. Turning to face him again, she said, 'I only asked you what it was, not to do it.'

He leaned forward, his hands clasped between his spread knees. 'Easier to do it than describe it. But – it'd fix 'em.'

'What's the price, then?' she asked.

'You are.'

She looked away, and felt her face turn hot. She knew what he meant, but, of course, he was just making fun of her. It was always a great joke, to find the ugliest girl and pretend you were in love with her.

'They all laugh at you,' she said. 'They say you're a merchant banker. They think you're an idiot.'

'I know they do,' he said.

'You only come from Wolverhampton.'

'Yeah,' he said.

'And you call yourself a witch.'

He got up, climbed on to the stage and seated himself behind the drum kit. With all the light in the room pooled around the bar, he was almost in darkness. Picking up the sticks, he began beating out, softly, complicated and changing rhythms. The people at the bar glanced round when he first began, but soon lost interest. Sheila climbed on to the stage too, and went close.

The Wiz began to chant, softly, only loud enough to be heard by her. 'Hear me,' he said, and touched the cymbal with a soft, scratching rattle. 'Hear me, all you—' A soft rattle, as of dry bones. 'Hear me, all you murdered, lying unfound, unfound in unfound graves.' Sheila glanced over her shoulder towards the bar where the only lights shone. The men and women gathered there, in the dim yellow pools of light, seemed separated from her by walls of dusk. The drumsticks rattled roundly, rhythmically. 'Come all you self-killed, trapped here on Earth, pacing out your time: come to me. Come and dance to my drum. All you spirits, lost and angry, all you lost and unfound—' The Wiz broke off and looked at Sheila, grinned at her because, despite herself, she looked scared. His face was distorted by the smudged paint on it.

'Not so simple as that,' he admitted. 'But—' He reached out and touched her shoulder. Drawing his hand away, he drew with it a long hair that showed light in the darkness. It wasn't her hair. As her eyes followed along its length, and met his, she realised that it was Kelly's hair, caught on her from the scuffle in the toilets. Kelly had long, fair hair. 'Give me a couple of days,' the Wiz said. Attacking the drums suddenly, he beat out a rapid, loud passage. 'The worst,' he said, 'are the ghosts of them who've killed theirselves.' Another rapid drumming, bringing shouts of protest from the other side of the darkness, from the bar. The Wiz ignored them. 'They kill theirselves to get back at people. And when they'm dead . . .' One drumstick beat out a slow, monotonous beat that quickly began to get on Sheila's nerves. 'They still want to get back at people.' A final crash of the cymbal, making her blink. 'A couple of days. How about a down-payment?' And he leaned over, leaned too close, smelling of beer and sweat.

Sheila pulled back sharply, jumped down from the stage and went to stand by her father. 'Hello!' he said, as if he'd forgotten that she was with him. 'Shall we be pushing off? Let me just have a word with Angelo . . .'

Without mentioning Kelly, she told her father something of what the Wiz had said on their way home – the stuff about the ghosts of the murdered and the self-killed. Her father had laughed. 'That's just his kind of stuff. He's a bullshitter.'

It had been comforting to hear her father say that. And comforting to arrive home at their untidy, ordinary house, with her mother offering to make them a cup of tea. Later, she was glad she'd met the Wiz. It was interesting to find that there were such people in the world. And he'd seemed to find her attractive. Perhaps he really had?

But just in case she got to feeling too pleased with herself, there was the knowledge that she had to go back to school next week, and Kelly and her friends would be there. Every day would be an endurance test. For another five weeks, until the end of term.

But Kelly just hadn't seemed her old self, after half-term. The very first time she'd seen Sheila – and Sheila had stiffened – Kelly had turned away and hurried off in the other direction, as if Kelly was the bullied one. Kelly's friends had tried to carry on the tradition of tormenting Sheila, but without Kelly it hadn't been as much fun; and it had died away. Sheila found herself coming and going from school, and making her way around school, without any interference. It had been wonderful.

And now Kelly was dead. 'I can fix it,' the Wiz had said, 'for a price.'

That night Sheila dreamed that she was kissed. And woke. And was afraid to go to sleep again.

Coming Home Late

I was watching a film on the television the other night. It was about a haunted house, and it had these people running around screaming their heads off because bloody arms were bursting through the walls and gripping them by the throat, and rotting corpses were taking up all the comfy chairs in the lounge. And I kept thinking: it's not like that. Hauntings aren't like that at all.

When I was a student, I got interested in modern folklore: all those stories which everyone swears happened to their friend, or their second cousin – the Chinese Take-Away that served stir-fried Alsatian; the doberman that choked on a burglar's fingers, the painting bought from a chain-store that brings a curse into the house with it – that sort of thing. I began to collect them from people, and write them down, with the date that I heard it, and the name of the person who told me it. And then I got to hear, through the family grapevine, that my own grandparents were spreading a new story. So I took my little tape-recorder and I went over to see them.

Gran immediately put the kettle on, and got some biscuits out, and I wedged my little tape-recorder in amongst the saucers, the sugar-bowl and the bottle of milk. I put a cassette in the machine, and got it all ready: play and record pressed down and the pause button on. 'Tell me about what happened to your neighbour,' I said.

'But you already know,' said Gran.

'He wants you to tell it into his recorder,' Grandad said.

'Oh, well,' Gran said, looking at the machine doubtfully. 'There isn't much to tell. Her was a lovely girl, though, wasn't her, Horace?'

'Lovely girl,' Grandad said.

'I'd see her most days, have a few words. Is it recording?' She leant forward and looked. 'Oh yes, the little wheels are going round. Her was ever so friendly, always smiling, always laughing – wasn't her, Horace?'

'Lovely smile,' Grandad said.

'Her used to work – what was the place? He'd have passed it on his way here—'

'The Warehouse,' Grandad said. I had passed it. A long building that had once been a warehouse, but had been turned into a nightclub. Its name was spelled out along its side, each letter a different colour, the colours already grubby and the yellow ones fading from sight.

'One of them nightclub places,' Gran said. 'They was always having trouble there – well, help yourself to a biscuit, Michael. You don't have to be polite here.'

I took a biscuit, to make her happy. 'Have more than that,' Grandad said. 'Have handful. I wouldn't be allowed to have 'em if you wasn't here.'

'Hark at him, making out I mistreat him. It was in the papers the other night, wasn't it, Horace? A brawl outside? And her used to come home so late. Ever so late. It used to be half-past two, getting on for three some mornings. No buses then, of course, so her had to walk – and her was followed.' Gran leaned forward and lowered her voice. 'On several occasions.'

'You mean, by men?' I asked.

'By men.' Gran nodded, her mouth crimped.

'Up to no good,' Grandad said.

'It used to frighten her. I said to her, "Well, why work there, Lisa? There must be other jobs," I said. Her said, "There ain't, Mrs Espley, not round here." Her said, "I'm lucky to have this one, and I ain't letting it go, not likely," her says. So I says to her, I says, "You know me and Horace hear you come in most nights." 'Cos me and Horace we'm light sleepers.' She leant forward and laid her hand on my arm. 'We don't need as much sleep as young uns like you!' She leant back and laughed. 'We go to bed, you know, and we doze off, and we wake up, and we have a little natter, and we doze off again – and we always wake up if the other one wakes up, don't we, love?'

'I usually get up and make a pot of tea about three o'clock,' Grandad said.

'That's right! He's a good sort, really . . . So you see, we often heard her come in. We'd hear her come up the street from a long way off, because – you know these young girls – her always used to wear these high-heeled shoes, what! Six inch heels they had, if they was an inch. I don't know how her could wear 'em, but you could certainly hear her coming. Tap, tap, tap, all up the street – 'cos, course, there ain't much noise at that time in the morning. Then we'd hear her shove the door open down there, and we'd hear her come up the steps and along the landing – and her'd stop outside her door while her got her keys sorted out – and then we'd hear her door slam. So I said to her, I said, "Me and Horace am awake most nights, and we'll listen out for you," I said. "We'll listen and we'll hear you shut the door, and we'll know you're home safe – and if anybody's following you," I said, "and if you'm scared, you just give a good yell. You just scream your head off," I said, "and me and Horace'll hear, and we'll phone the police." 'Cos we've got a phone by our bed – you know, your mother had it put in, Michael, so it wouldn't be any trouble to phone 'em. And when I told Horace what I'd said, he went across and saw her hisself—'

Embarrassed, Grandad coughed. 'I said, if her give a good scream if somebody was following her, I'd come out and see him off. June can phone the police, I said, but what you want is somebody to come down and see 'em off. Her said that made her feel a lot better.'

'Well, it did, I know it did,' Gran said. 'Because her hadn't got all that far to come from the nightclub, you see. And it made her feel better to think that somebody was listening out for her. Horace used to bring our old poker to bed with him, so it was to hand.'

'All it's good for now the council've put in gas-fires,' Grandad said.

'I used to say to her, "We heared you come in last night," just so her'd know we had been listening out. And her bought us that lovely plant for Christmas, didn't her, Horace? A poinsettia. Her said it was a thank-you, but I said, there's no need for that. I said, "We've got a granddaughter, and we'd like to think that somebody'd do the same for her." Well, that's what makes the world go round, isn't it? It's nothing special, needing thank-yous. But her used to buy us little things like that just the same. Her was a lovely girl.'

Grandad nodded soberly, in agreement.

'And then, when it happened,' Gran said, 'it wasn't somebody who'd followed her home from the nightclub at all. It was just two bits of kids. And we never heard a thing, even though we was just across the landing.'

'What did happen exactly?' I asked.

'Well, we only know what was in the papers, like

everybody else,' Gran said. 'And a little bit that the police told us . . .' She seemed to have lost her zest for telling the story, and looked at Grandad instead.

'It was a Friday afternoon it happened,' he said. 'They used to pay her on a Thursday, see. And these two kids come to see her, wanting some money. Her knowed 'em, it seems like. So her let 'em in, you see. There wasn't a struggle or any shouting for us to hear. They got in because her let 'em in. They was only seventeen or sixteen, a chap and a wench. I don't know their names. They was in all the papers, but I don't remember things like that. I ain't interested in their names: I think they should have been hung. Anyway, they asked her to give 'em some money, or so they said, and her wouldn't. So they said. But her'd have give anybody anything; her was a lovely girl.'

'That's right,' Gran said.

'I think they was just sadists,' said Grandad. 'They wanted to hurt her; that's what I think.'

'Ooh, it was terrible,' said Gran.

'They hit her with hammer. Banged her over the head with hammer; not just once—'

'Don't, Horace.'

'Dozens of times,' Grandad went on. 'And stabbed her, with one of her own knives out the kitchen. The bastards.'

'And we never heard anything,' Gran said. 'That's

what I can't understand. Only just across the landing, and we didn't hear her shout, we didn't hear any uproar – we didn't hear nothing.'

'Well,' I said. 'It's understandable. If her door was shut, and your door was shut – and there was traffic going by outside, and lots of people about – and you had your television on . . .'

'We did,' Gran said eagerly. 'We'd have had the telly on.'

'And if – sorry, but if your hearing's not what it was – I mean, high-heeled shoes on a hard pavement at three o'clock in the morning, that's a nice sharp, clear sound that'd carry well. You'd hear that. But picking out a few thumps and shouts from all the other noises going on in a normal afternoon – that's a different matter.'

'That's right,' Grandad agreed. 'Anyway, the papers said her died almost instantly from one of the stab wounds, so her didn't make all that much noise. I keep telling her that, but her won't have it.'

'I just can't believe we didn't hear *anything*,' Gran said.

'Did you find the body?' I asked.

'No, the police did that. We just noticed her wasn't about. I didn't see her during the day, and I usually did . . . and we didn't hear her go off to work, or come home. And then her milk stood outside all day – her didn't have much milk delivered, just a couple of bottles a week. But this one bottle stood outside all day. And then your mother come visiting on the Sunday, and I said to her, I said, "We haven't seen that young girl who lives opposite for days." Well, it wasn't since the Friday, was it Horace? And your mother says, "You should go and find out if her's all right." And I says, "Well, I will, in a bit." "No, in a bit about it," says your mother – well, you know what her's like – "let's go and find out now."'

'Rotten busybody,' Grandad said proudly.

'Well, your mother goes across the landing, and I goes with her, and we knocked and knocked on that door, and we couldn't get any answer. Course,' said the old lady, leaning forward and looking into my eyes, 'that's because the poor wench was lying dead in there. It makes me go cold to think about that. Me and your mother knocking outside and her lying in there dead. Well, after a bit, your mother says we should phone the police. I thought that was a bit drastic, meself. I thought, well, it's only been a couple of days. I should have left it a bit longer meself, but it just goes to show, don't it? A good job your mother was here, I suppose. It was a young copper turned up – only about twenty, he was – and he asked a lot of questions about when we'd last seen her, and what her usually did, and so on. And then he went and hammered on the door – he really knocked, he did – didn't he, Horace?'

'Hammered it down, nigh on,' Grandad said. 'I

should have thought he'd have raised the dead.'

'Horace!' Grandad smiled to himself, and Gran turned to me again. 'Course, there wasn't no answer. So he called out some other policemen, and they come and they knocked the door in. And then, of course, they found her. In the living room, they said, blood all over the place. They wouldn't let us see, and I didn't want to. They didn't have to fight to keep me out. They wouldn't have got me in there. Oh, I couldn't believe it when they told me. I mean, you read it in the papers, and you see it in the news, but when it happens next door . . . You don't know what to think. I kept thinking about that poor young girl – I kept thinking, maybe her'd shouted for help and we'd never heard her.'

Gran's voice became thinner and more thready, and I felt my own throat getting tighter in sympathy with her distress. I would have put in some question to help her over this part of the story, except I didn't want to discover that my own voice was shaky.

'I kept thinking that her'd relied on us to listen out for her, and when her'd really needed us, we hadn't heard anything.'

'It was just one of them things,' Grandad said. 'Not our fault. We'd have done what we could if we had heard – but what could we have done? Two youngsters with a knife and an hammer. They'd have killed we an' all.'

'All we could do was make tea for the police,' Gran

said, with a sudden brightening. 'Her flat was full of police for days. They was searching it for evidence . . . They all used to come into here for tea. It was like running a canteen.'

'Her spent we pension in biscuits for 'em,' Grandad said.

'But they was lovely. They had a whip-round and bought us a bottle of whisky, you know, to thank us for all the tea and sandwiches and that.'

I nodded. They seemed to be talking for the sake of cheering themselves up; or perhaps they didn't want to get on to the next part of the story, the part I'd really come to hear.

'When did all this happen?' I asked, although I knew.

'Oh – it'd be – getting on for a year now.'

After considering, Grandad said, 'Seven or eight months ago, I'd say.'

'No – a year, Horace. Longer.'

I asked, 'And when did you first hear—?'

'Oh, not while the police was here,' Gran said. 'Not until a while after they'd gone. Let's see . . . It was more than a week afterwards, wasn't it? It was after they'd boarded her door up.'

'More like two weeks.'

'He'd gone to make a cup of tea as usual.' Gran's voice became quieter, her words slower. 'So it'd be about three in the morning, I suppose. And I heard her coming home.' She widened her eyes at me, and nodded solemnly as she repeated, 'I heard her coming home.'

'I heard it an' all,' Grandad said. 'Footsteps. In high heels. Tap, tap, tap.'

'All up the street,' said Gran, 'and turning in here. I heard the door open downstairs, and I heard her come up the steps – and of course, I thought it was somebody going up to the top floor, but they come along the landing outside here. So then I thought it was somebody going along to the end flat. But it stopped outside the door of her flat. But' – she wagged her finger at me – 'I've never heard the door of her flat slam like we used to. They always stop outside the flat, the footsteps just end there. We never hear nothing after that.'

'And what makes you think it isn't just a woman coming home?' I said.

'How many women come home to here at three in the morning?' Gran said scornfully. 'In high heels. And they always come in here, and up the steps, and they always stop outside her flat. Always. Horace'll tell you.'

I looked at Grandad and he nodded. 'I know her step,' he said. 'You can laugh if you like. I know I've never believed in anything like it meself, but what you hear with your own ears you've got to believe, and I ain't ashamed to say it. I've heard 'em. I'd come to recognise her footsteps, and I'm telling you it's her, even though her's dead.'

It's a strange feeling when people you know and love, and who you know are telling you the truth, tell you something that you can't believe. I asked, 'Has anybody else in the flats heard her?'

'I don't know,' Gran said. 'I'd feel daft asking them. But anyway, they're young. They sleep sound. They never heard her coming home when she was alive, let alone—' She broke off and laughed at herself. 'Well, don't it sound silly to say, let alone now, when her's dead?'

'If you hear it, you hear it,' Grandad said. 'If somebody has told me they heard a ghost coming home every night, I should have said, "What you take me for, a fool?" But I *do* hear her; and I know it's her. So that's that.'

'Why don't you stay the night?' Gran suddenly asked. 'Then you can tape-record her!'

'You can't record a ghost,' I said.

'Ever tried?'

'No,' I said, 'but . . .'

'I can make you up a bed on the settee,' Gran said. 'No trouble. You'll be comfortable there.'

I didn't really want to stay, but it was no use arguing. Gran had made up her mind. She fetched blankets out, and pillows, and made up a bed on the settee, and I gave in. We spent the rest of the evening watching the television, eating biscuits, drinking tea and chatting, until ten o'clock, when Gran and Grandad went to bed. No wonder they were always awake at three in the morning.

I watched television by myself for a while, but I felt guilty about wasting their electricity, so I soon switched it off, and the fire, and read old magazines by the light of a lamp. The dim light tired my eyes, and the room quickly cooled once the fire was turned off. So it probably wasn't much after eleven when I switched off the lamp, pulled the blankets over me, and settled down to sleep myself.

Gran woke me, shaking me and repeating my name. The electric light was on, glaring in my eyes when I could open them, which was only with difficulty and not for very long. My face felt cold and stiff, and I couldn't make sense of what she was saying because my head was buzzing with something about Sir Arthur Conan Doyle and teacups and a deerstalker hat . . . Taking tea with Sir Arthur, that was it; and he was wearing his deerstalker cap – only it wasn't his, it was Sherlock Holmes' . . .

Gran, her short, fat figure bundled up in a lime-green housecoat, and with purple fluffy slippers on her feet, was standing by me. 'I can't remember the last time I slept like that,' she said. 'Your Grandad'll bring you a cup of tea in a minute.'

I sat up and blinked, and managed to bring things together. I could hear Grandad in the kitchen of the little flat, moving about. The sounds had that peculiar, flat, early-morning quality; and the electric light was bleak, dim and harsh, as electric light is when it's pitch-dark outside.

'I thought I'd wake you up so you could have a cup of tea before she comes,' Gran said, 'but I didn't think I'd have to spend ten minutes shaking you. Listen.'

For a moment I didn't know what I was supposed to be listening for. I heard a car go by slowly: God knows where it was coming from or going to at that time in the morning. I looked at Gran's upraised finger and bright eyes for some clue, but she only mouthed again: 'Listen!'

I concentrated. The only sound I could hear, very faintly, was someone walking, someone far off as yet. But though distant and quiet, the sound was very clear and definite: tap, tap, tap – the sound of high-heeled shoes. My face must have registered that I'd heard, because Gran said, 'That's her!'

Grandad came in with mugs of tea, and, still feeling cold and stiff – and very hungry – I thanked him fervently as I took mine. If you have to be awake at three in the morning, listening to ghosts walking in the street outside, it's good to have a big mug of hot tea to be awake with. Grandad stood listening to the footsteps too, and nodding. 'That's her.'

I moved over to the window with my tea. I drew the curtains aside and looked down into the street. The little flat was on the first floor, and I would have had a good view of the street approaching it, if it had been light. As it was, I had to press my forehead against the cold glass before I could begin to pick out, in shades of grey, the edge of the pavement and the lampposts. But I was certain that if anyone was walking down there, I would see something of them. There was no one; but then the footsteps were still some way off – getting louder as they drew nearer, but I wouldn't have expected to see the person making them just yet.

But the footsteps came closer and closer until I could no longer make that excuse. Definite, distinct; and now, besides the tap, tap, tap of the heels, I could hear the occasional scuff of the sole, the little screeches as the edge of the heel dragged along the pavement. I pressed my face against the window glass, bending my nose as I peered into the darkness of the street. I should have been able to see something of the woman walking down there, but I could make out nothing but darkness, shadows and the vague shapes of cars, and lampposts. Perhaps it was too dark; perhaps I was being dazzled by the light in the room behind me.

At that moment, from beneath us, there came the unmistakable sound of the block's heavy door being buffeted open by a hefty shove. There could be no doubt that the door had opened. We heard the soft thud of a body hitting it; we heard the hinges turn; we heard the metal that coated the lower section of the door scratch on the concrete floor. I turned away from the window and grinned at Gran and Grandad. The sound was so loud, and was so obviously made by solid things, that I had no doubt that someone real and living had made it.

'It's always like that,' Gran said, and picked up my tape-recorder. 'Quick! Or you'll be too late!'

I smiled, but, to please her, I took the tape-recorder and, moving quickly, I fitted a spare tape into it as I moved to the door of their flat. I opened the door, went out on to the narrow, dark, concrete landing, and set the recorder down on the floor outside the boarded-up door of the flat opposite. I pressed down the record and play buttons, and withdrew to the open doorway behind me.

The light from the doorway split apart the darkness of the landing and threw my shadow over the grey concrete and the planks that covered the opposite door. The footsteps were coming up the stairs from the landing below. I watched the stairway, confidently waiting for the appearance of the woman who was making them. In a little patch of light, my tape-recorder hissed softly.

Clack, clack: the flat, sharp sound of high-heeled shoes on concrete steps, climbing higher and coming nearer. I was listening as hard as I've ever listened to anything, and I could hear other sounds: I could hear the soft sound of slightly out-of-breath breathing, the breathing of a woman who had hurried along a lonely street and then climbed a flight of stairs. I could hear the sound the rough weave of her stockings made, and the sound her skirt made against her stockings. There was a little slap as one shoe partly left her foot, a scrape as the toe of the other foot slid along the surface of a step. And clack, clack, clack all the time.

But no woman appeared on the stairway. I began to experience that strange, displaced sensation that comes when your senses contradict each other; and the top of my head seemed to be gently lifting off. My ears told me plainly that the woman had now climbed so high up the stairs that she was within my sight. They told me that the clarity of the sounds was such that there could be no doubt. But my eyes told me, as plainly, that there was no woman on the stairway. My eyes were straining painfully in their sockets as I searched the air for the shape I knew had to be there, searched for it with intensity – and saw nothing but the concrete walls, the concrete floor and stairway, half-lit by the light from my grandparents' flat.

The footsteps paused at the stop of the stairs. The woman was standing in the light, but there was no woman. In that moment of silence, I drifted from the door of the flat and crossed the landing to stand by the boarded-up door, near the recorder. My soft trainers didn't make much noise: what noise they did make would be easily distinguishable from the clacking of the high heels – if the tape picked up that sound.

The footsteps started again. I was directly in their path, but I still couldn't make out who was making them. Which was utterly impossible. The footsteps were loud, echoing back from the concrete walls. They were *present*, there, with me, shaking the air. I could hear the little wobbles as the woman balanced on the tiny heels. Clack, clack, scuff, clack, clack, right up to where I stood.

I was scared. My body was scared all by itself, without my having to do any thinking. My heart bumped up its rate, and breathing became harder. I felt my blood withdrawing from my face, and the flesh of my face hardening. But I stayed where I was. My fist clenched against the wall where it rested, but I stayed where I was. The footsteps came right up to me. If there had been anyone there, we should have been nose to nose. But there was only cold. I felt the cold approach. Perhaps it was only my fear, but I felt that I was standing in the blast of air from a cold-store. I felt my cheekbones, my nose, my eyes chill: the skin of my chest, my nipples, hands, the fronts of my thighs were touched with cold.

The footsteps stopped. It was standing there in front of me, invisible. Was it waiting? Looking at me?

My heart rate went up another notch until it was painful. I wanted to get away from it, but I think I was too scared to move. And then I heard another sound, one that nearly did for me. It was a dull rattle, a chink, and then a fine, steely ringing. The sound of a handbag being rummaged through, and a couple of keys on a ring being lifted out. I knew exactly that chime of jangling keys.

I sank at the knees, I went down, I knelt. When I realised I was kneeling I looked up at the rough boards covering the door, at the concrete corner of the door-frame, and I thought: am I kneeling at her feet? But there was no one there.

I waited, holding my breath, to hear the key go into the lock, to hear it turn and the door open – but there was nothing more. After that thin little noise, that jangling of keys, there was nothing more. I could feel the concrete pressing the seams of my jeans against my knee-bone, and my lungs began to hurt as much as my racing heart, but I heard nothing more from the ghost. Maybe the blood thumping in my head and making it ache drowned out all other sounds – until I heard my gran call me.

I looked round as if I was coming out of a trance. Gran was leaning out from her doorway. Grandad was peering over her head.

I stared at them dazedly. Then, stiff with fright and cold, I got slowly to my feet and walked – tottered – towards them. I'd forgotten my tape-recorder. I went back for it, stooping so clumsily I almost fell over.

As Gran shut the door of the flat behind us, I was rewinding the tape. I put the recorder on the table, sat down on their settee, and began to shake all over.

'Oh dear, oh dear. Fetch him another cup of tea, Horace,' Gran said.

'I'm OK, I'm OK,' I said. I picked up the tape-recorder and, after several tries because of my shaking hands, pressed the play button. The tape ran, buzzing for a few moments, then there was the sound of the record button being depressed, and the slight scuffling sounds of my retreat across the landing. The sound had that strangeness that recorded sounds do: a little unreal, almost rehearsed.

The tape ran quietly for a while after that – but then we heard the footsteps coming up the stairs again, coming closer and closer, louder and louder – though on the tape their sharp clear quality was a little distorted, a little muffled.

A quieter, softer tread – that was me in my trainers – and then the last few steps of the high-heeled shoes. Then silence: my fear didn't record on tape. And Gran's voice, sounding so strange to her own ears that it made her laugh: 'Michael?' More silence; and then the dull clink of the machine being switched off.

I stopped it again, and rewound the tape.

'Well! You did get it on tape, you see!' Gran said.

'Why?' I said. 'Why does she come back?'

Gran said, 'Why was her murdered, poor wench?'

And that's all the explanation there's ever likely to be. Take it from me, that's what they're like, real hauntings. All it needs to bring you to your knees in suffocating fear, is the sound of walking and the jingle of a bunch of keys.

Earthfasts

William Mayne

It started with a noise reverberating in the hill. David and Keith see a boy appear from the ground, carrying a candle and beating a drum. A boy from another time who will have an irreversible effect on both their lives.

Extraordinary things start to happen. Standing stones move. Giants stalk the hill. Wild boar rampage through the town.

Then David vanishes. And Keith must search through time for his friend.

h HODDER *Another Hodder Children's book*

Waterbound

Jane Stemp

The City is a place of rules, a place where Admin is always watching . . . a place where there is no room to be different.

Under the City, the river flows from light into dark, into an unknown place. A place which hides a secret. Something forbidden – out of sight and out of mind.

There Gem finds the Waterbound, the children the City forgot. She joins in their fight to be part of the world she knows.

Why are they underground? Is there a way out?

ORDER FORM

0 340 65327 2	**EARTHFASTS** *William Mayne*	£3.99	☐
0 340 65126 1	**CRADLEFASTS** *William Mayne*	£3.99	☐
0 340 63477 4	**WATERBOUND** *Jane Stemp*	£3.99	☐
0 340 63478 2	**FOUNDLING** *June Oldham*	£3.99	☐

All Hodder Children's books are available at your local bookshop or newsagent, or can be ordered direct from the publisher. Just tick the titles you want and fill in the form below. Prices and availability subject to change without notice.

Hodder Children's Books, Cash Sales Department, Bookpoint, 39 Milton Park, Abingdon, OXON, OX14 4TD, UK. If you have a credit card you may order by telephone – 01235 831700.

Please enclose a cheque or postal order made payable to Bookpoint Ltd to the value of the cover price and allow the following for postage and packing: UK & BFPO: £1.00 for the first book, 50p for the second book and 30p for each additional book ordered up to a maximum charge of £3.00.
OVERSEAS & EIRE: £2.00 for the first book, £1.00 for the second book and 50p for each additional book.

Name ....

Address ....

....

....

If you would prefer to pay by credit card, please complete:
Please debit my Visa/Access/Diner's Card/American Express (delete as applicable) card no:

Signature ....

Expiry Date ....